For Joy ~ with
deep gratitude for
your work, your
words, your teaching,
and your inspiration!

from
Andrew

Fragments

of the Brooklyn Talmud

Fragments
of the Brooklyn Talmud

ANDREW RAMER

AFTERWORD BY RABBI DAVID WOLPE

RESOURCE *Publications* · Eugene, Oregon

FRAGMENTS OF THE BROOKLYN TALMUD

Resource Publications
An Imprint of Wipf and Stock Publishers
199 W. 8th Ave., Suite 3
Eugene, OR 97401

www.wipfandstock.com

PAPERBACK ISBN: 978-1-5326-6328-4
HARDCOVER ISBN: 978-1-5326-6329-1
EBOOK ISBN: 978-1-5326-6330-7

Manufactured in the U.S.A.   01/10/19

Books by Andrew Ramer

From Wipf and Stock

Deathless

Torah Told Different

Revelations for a New Millennium

Queering the Text

Two Flutes Playing

The Spiritual Dimensions of Healing Addictions

& Further Dimensions of Healing Addictions—*with Donna Cunningham*

And

Angel Answers

Ask Your Angels—*with Alma Daniel and Timothy Wyllie*

For Irene Eber, who changed my life
in a Jerusalem classroom in 1971
and Isaac Kikawada, who changed my life
in a Berkeley classroom a year later.
Without you there would be no books.
Todah rabbah.

Contents

Whatever a disciple of the wise may propound
by way of explaining law in the most distant future
was already revealed to Moses on Mount Sinai.
The Jerusalem Talmud

Re-vision–the act of looking back, of seeing with fresh eyes,
of entering an old text from a new critical direction–
is for women more than a chapter in cultural history:
it is an act of survival.
Adrienne Rich

Overview

EIGHTY YEARS AGO, IN the final decade of the 21st century–a time of increasing social, economic, and environmental horrors–over two thousand rabbis from each of the seven streams of Judaism that had been practiced at that time gathered together in the city of Brooklyn under the leadership of Rabbi Sara-Rosa ibn Nuriel to create a new Talmud, one that would represent and teach, guide and encourage, that would assemble and codify their Aggadah and Halachah–their stories and legal decisions–for Jews in the surviving communities around the world.

Rabbi Sara-Rosa's father was a direct descendant of the 18th century Persian rabbi and translator Baba'i ibn Nuriel, while her mother was a descendant of his illustrious contemporary, the Eastern European founder of Hasidism, the Baal Shem Tov. Sara-Rosa ibn Nuriel was educated in a girl's yeshiva in Los Angeles, did her undergraduate studies at the Sorbonne and her graduate work in anthropology in Tehran. Some years after returning to North America she joined and was ordained in the path of the newest of Jewish streams, the post-Orthodox movement founded in Brooklyn by Rabbi Moshe-Leah m'beit Goldberg. That path was called Deconstructionist Judaism by its detractors and Edenic Judaism by its founder, whose successor Rabbi Carla Sarfati was Sara-Rosa's mentor, and who she eventually followed as the third leader of Edenic Judaism.

In that time of horrors, both global and in the Jewish world, following massive fires and the largest earthquake in California history, the evacuation of most of the Middle East due to a quarter of a century of drought and unlivable scorching heat, and a decade after the virulent MOT pandemic had wiped out one sixth of the Earth's population—it was Rabbi Sara-Rosa's background, plus her great scholarly and spiritual experience, that empowered her to approach leaders from all of the often-hostile strands of Jewish practice to gather together in Brooklyn. Their shared intention was to create a unified code of behavior and beliefs that would be grounded in tradition and yet inclusive of modern perspectives and contemporary modes of discourse and exploration. The call that Rabbi ibn Nuriel put out—for two ten-day gatherings a year to be held over the course of five years—was in part inspired by the Grand Sanhedrin that Napoleon convened in 1807 for Jews from every part of his empire to resolve the challenging issues of their time.

The rabbis, cantors, maggids, teachers, and scholars she welcomed to Brooklyn came from varied and divided Jewish communities that were still reeling from the nightmares of that period. With the end of the State of Israel and with so many clergy, teachers, and leaders lost to MOT, we can only imagine the ways in which those shared nightmares helped to focus and gradually unite them. We know that all of the gatherings met in closed sessions, their proceedings and the materials they brought and crafted deliberately contained on a private linked non-wireless network as they moved toward codifying a final public document during the tenth and final gathering.

From a brief surviving account of their meetings, found in a z-mail from Rabbi Sara-Rosa to Shimona Abouav, the first and last Mizrahi chief rabbi of Israel, we know that there were approximately 7700 Jewish sages still alive in the world. More than 2200 of them made their way to Brooklyn from every part of the world, as Rabbi ibn Nuriel felt strongly that the Talmud they created needed to come from actual meetings and not just from ongoing wave-net contact. The ten sessions were all held in the Eden Synagogue, which stood on a high point above the rising waters—for Brooklyn had become the vital center of world Jewry after the evacuation of the Middle East.

Wanting the Talmud they created to be not just a footnote or very late echo of the Babylonian and Jerusalem Talmuds, the sages who met in Brooklyn were committed to crafting a work in multiple genres and media. In addition to the Halachic and Aggadic texts we would expect in such a work, Rabbi Sara-Rosa put out a call for stories, poems, and letters, for essays and sermons, as well as art and audio and video materials, with the dream of crafting a "common language"–that phrase coming from the title of a seminal book and poem written by the 20th century Jewish American lesbian poet Adrienne Rich. We know too that there were representatives in attendance from many other faith traditions, including active and engaged Buddhist and Muslim caucuses, but only one surviving document reflects their input—on Global Healing—and we know nothing about their contributions or about their wider role in the gatherings.

The Talmud project was controversial, both for including such a range of Jewish, non-Jewish, and multi-faith Jewish voices, and coming as it did more than a millennia and a half after the codification of the Babylonian and Jerusalem Talmuds. We also know that as the roots of the Mishnah and the two ancient Talmuds emerged from the ruins of the Second Temple, the failure of the Bar Kochba revolt, and from centuries of trauma, that this new Talmud project was a response to the escalating threats to human survival, which have only grown more dire in the years since the ten Talmud convocations were held. In another extant z-mail, sent by Rabbi Sara-Rosa to her former wife in Beijing after the ninth assembly, she mentions that a solid working draft of the project–more than 15,000 pages long–in eighteen languages–had been compiled. We know too from that z-mail that thousands of visual images, over 800 hours of video materials, and over 3000 hours of audio materials including interviews as well as thousands of songs and prayers had also been collected, to be used in ways that can only be imagined. For alas, as we all know–the tenth and

3

final gathering of our revered sages had just begun–when New York City was destroyed in a nuclear attack.

The survivors of Edenic Judaism eventually regrouped in the hills of Oakland, California, where a small thriving synagogue and academy exist to this day, but it was assumed by them and others that everything the scholars and sages collected had been lost. But miraculously, two years ago–a single laptop was discovered by an archaeological team working in the now-submerged and still-radioactive ruins of the Eden Synagogue in Brooklyn. The laptop had been only slightly damaged in the blast that destroyed the city, but it had been sitting under water for more than a decade, so none of us expected there to be any remaining information on it–but in the hard-drive of that battered laptop our digitographers discovered a very small number of files that were intact from the vast amount of material that had been assembled.

As you read through these pages you will surely feel as we feel, both a great delight that anything has survived–all of it in English, the dominant spoken language of the convocations–along with a deep aching sorrow that none of the rest of the text or any of the audio or visual materials were retrievable, save for one verse only of a single song, titled "Ark-less," which we have placed at the very end of the book. We pause now to honor those millions who perished in the blast and to remember its consequences for all of our people and for all of humanity. May their memories be for a blessing.

One of our hopes, as we slowly made our way through the digital fragments, was that we would find a text called *The Five Books of Mona,* written by Rabbi Lydia Nakamura Ramer, which was mentioned in z-mails as one of the works that might be included in the Talmud. A retelling of the Torah, we know that the flood story was told through Hurricane Katrina, which struck the city of New Orleans in the year 2005, and the Babel story through the second destruction of the World Trade Center in New York in 2085. Rabbi Nakamura Ramer's son Max, a dancer living in Paris, said in an interview with the *Jewish Nightly Forward,* that for Moses's mysterious death and unknown grave his mother had Mona hiking on Mount Shasta in Northern California when she was carried off in a space ship, from which she could see all of Planet Earth turning beneath her–so you can imagine our immense thrill when we came upon a file with the book in it! Alas, as you shall see, only the very beginning survives, which parallels the opening verses of Genesis, along with a few later fragments.

You may recall that there were only three survivors of the Talmud project. Hazzan Ari McDaniels from Dublin was in Nairobi at the time of the bombing, visiting a sick relative. Till the end of his life he refused to talk about the Talmud, as did Rabbi Yaun Ling Chen from Stockholm, who was at a meditation retreat in Hawaii and due back in New York the day before the tenth session began, but was detained there because of inclement weather. Rabbi Tina-Rob Cohen from Australia was at the first eight gatherings but not at the rest as she was in her late nineties and descending into Alzheimer's. Historians question the notes she left behind. In them she spoke of "The Holy City of Brooklyn," conjuring in our minds a new Jerusalem or a new Safed. It was she who called the great unfinished work begun there "The Brooklyn Talmud," the name by which it has been known for the last eighty years, although in what appears to be an introduction to the text we find that its contributors called it–"A Global Talmud."

We ache to see everything that had been gathered and ache to see how those texts would have informed our lives in this increasingly bleak time if they had all survived. Given the fragmentary nature of the texts that we could read, we arranged the ones that follow without trying to put them into any of the six Orders mentioned in that introduction, as many if not most of them could belong in more than one. Further, we have no idea which, if any, of the surviving fragments would have actually made it into the completed Talmud, or if they even reflect the larger values the assembled sages were intending to codify. For example, there are several pieces on the Shechinah. Were they meant to rectify the male- and Male-focused slant of our older texts, or is their survival simply an accident? We may never know. But what you find below is everything that we could extract and reconstruct, including a series of stories by an otherwise unknown maggid, Beata Roman, which were found in individual files in various locations on the hard drive. Rather than put them all together, we've scattered them here as well, assuming that that was the intention of the Talmud's creators, to use them, perhaps, as midrashic punctuation.

This collection of fragments is dedicated to Rabbi Sara-Rosa ibn Nuriel, to the sages mentioned above, and to all of the many other named and unnamed leaders in their communities who attended the working sessions and whose final life's project was their and our unfinished Talmud. May these fragments of a corpus whose lingering ghost haunts us to this day, in the scattered communities in which Jews still survive on our battered, degraded, once-beautiful planet, bring us comfort and meaning, wisdom and guidance, in what we hope will not be our final days.

Malka Christina Faraj & Carlos Steinberg-Greenberg
Retrieval Editors, Hebrew University, Antarctica City

The Surviving Texts

A Global Talmud

By Rabbi Sara-Rosa ibn Nuriel

In the first session of our convocation we agreed unanimously that we would build our work upon the great *Mishnah* compiled in antiquity by our spiritual ancestor Rabbi Judah the Prince. He organized his material in six orders and we agreed that we would follow that organizational structure, extrapolating from it for our time. His *Mishnah* rose up in the century after the destruction of an independent Jewish homeland and the leveling of our last temple, followed by another century of harsh overlords. We who gathered in Brooklyn agreed that following the end of another independent Jewish state and in a time of global destruction and the possibility of the end of human life, that a new code is required by those of our people who have survived.

What follows is an outline of the six Orders of the material we gathered during our first nine meetings, of stories and texts in multiple formats and media. In six month's time we will gather together again to finalize our project, in the Name of the One who created us all.

Order One: **Questions**–We wonder about the nature of existence, we marvel at all growing things, and ask each other how to best plant, tend, and harvest in a degraded world, and we also ask how to dream and cultivate hope and nurture possibilities.

Order Two: **Beliefs**–Shabbat, our holy days, old and new, established and spontaneous; our varying notions of The Divine;

how to rejoice in dangerous times and how to celebrate even the smallest things when that's sometimes all that we have left.

Order Three: **Identities**–Women and men and people of all genders and sexualities, including stories and essays and poems, along with rabbinic statements on love, relationships, and families in our frightening time.

Order Four: **Challenges**–Dealing with civil and criminal law, the relationship between Jewish laws and customs and those of the dominant cultures in which we live, and how we relate to and integrate them into our lives.

Order Five: **Communities**–Our synagogues, minyanim, chavurot, kehillot; prayer, ritual, belief and multiple beliefs and non-belief in our communities; along with variant texts and traditions and how to interconnect them all for the survival of our people.

Order Six: **Practices**–The laws and customs of purity in a massively polluted world, including guidance on food, health, self-care, illness, death, burial, and our varied relationships to our toxic surroundings in times when the coming of a messiah seems long overdue.

Commenting on the First Chapter of *Pirke Avot*

BY RABBAH SALMA PRESTI OF
THE TEMPLE OF THE VINEYARD, MEXICO CITY

MOSES RECEIVED THE WRITTEN **Torah from Sinai, and transmitted it to Joshua, Joshua to the Elders, the elders to the Prophets, the Prophets to the Men of the Great Assembly**, who began the compilation of the Oral Torah, which they passed on to our ancestors. And we, in our time, we are creating a third Torah, to wrap around and weave through the other two, a new text which grows up from the other two, a Torah of the Heart, which we will pass on to those who live after us.

They, the Men of the Great Assembly, **said three things: "Be deliberate in judgment, develop many disciples, and make a fence for the Torah."** We say two things: Honor the wisdom of all the women and queers and marginal people who went before us, for they are the teachers of us all. And honor all the spirit traditions of the world, for they all have something to teach us about how to be a Jew and a human being in our damaged and damaging time.

Simon the Righteous was among the survivors of the Great Assembly. He used to say: "The world depends upon three things–on Torah study, on divine service, and on kind deeds." In this new Torah of the Heart we say four things: take care of your body, take care of the collective body of your extended family and community, take care of the body of the planet, and know that all of them are connected to the teeming universe and to That which we call by many names and think of and encounter in many different ways.

Huldah in Heaven

BY RACHEL KAUR KAHAN, THE CHIEF MAGGID OF INDIA

IT WAS ONE INDIGNITY after another. Watching the priests discard all of the scrolls of her work–not after she was gone, as she'd always expected, but as she lay ill on what soon became her deathbed. Her loyal servant Leah told her the horrible news.

"Everything?"

"Yes," Leah answered, "Everything."

"I was foolish," she thought, "to give all of God's words to me to the temple after His final revelation to me came last year."

That her children were all disappointments was something she was quite used to. Zebulon and his airs, Joram and his drinking, Zipporah, her lout of a husband, and all of those children running around speaking the most horrible jargon, as if their grandmother hadn't been one of the few women who'd been a prophet of the God of Israel. "I could count us," she thought to herself, as Leah wiped her sweaty brow. "But why bother?"

When she breathed her last breath, when the force of life in her body flew out and up from the very top of her head–which was a surprise, not something she'd ever expected. "From the top of my head and not from my heart is so unsettling," she thought, instantly liberated from her frail and ailing body. But in that very same moment she found herself surrounded by beings of light that she knew were angels. Four of them, but with no wings, no arms, no faces. In fact they weren't human at all–just great big pulsing spheres of light. And yes, they were loving, "But," she thought, "there is much warmth in a flame, but so little tenderness."

Heaven—they were there a moment later. But nothing was as she had thought it would be. The gates, if you could call them that, were made of light and not polished stone as she'd long imagined. And the courtyards stretching out for miles like those before a mighty temple—they too were made of light. For so long she'd yearned for something solid in the afterlife, something to make up for all of life's hardships and disappointments. Even her fame had been no comfort—for what true prophet really wants that job? No, all that Huldah had ever wanted was to be married to her husband Shallum and to raise good and happy children. God coming to her had not been anything she'd even once imagined—till it happened. And when she'd thought of death and of what came afterwards, she had—and perhaps it was vanity—imagined that like Moses she too would be able to see, if not all of God, at least a very little bit of Him.

How maddening, to do her best to be a good wife, good mother, good servant to the Voice that had first come to her all of those years ago—that when she finally stood before the great throne, a throne of all-encompassing light—what she saw seated upon that throne was not the bearded man she'd often imagined was the source of the Voice that came to her, nor even a woman of power like the goddess that so many of her women friends worshipped—but instead a tiny little golden weasel, sitting up on its hind legs and smiling at her. Another indignity, to have been created in Its image, for such was the meaning of her name: weasel—when she'd always interpreted and explained to her many students that the language of those verses in the Torah is not literal but metaphoric, imagistic, symbolic.

Four Good Friends

By Rabbi Sonia Rodriguez Rabinowitz,
Congregation Ain-Tamid, Vancouver, Canada

Four entered Paradise: Ben Azzai, Ben Zoma, Ben Abuya, and Rabbi Akiva. Ben Azzai gazed and died. Ben Zoma gazed and went mad. Ben Abuya became a heretic. Only Rabbi Akiva entered in peace and left in peace.

From *The Babylonian* and *The Jerusalem Talmuds*

FRAN, ALICE, DEBBIE, AND Susan met in an English class during their second year at Barnard, back in the days when you could still walk outside freely, without having to wear a breathing mask. They started doing their homework together, in a café across the street from the Cathedral of St. John the Divine, where they discovered that all of them were committed to making the world a better place by becoming teachers, all of them were sure that they were going to marry Jewish men, although none of them ever went to services, and pretty quickly they all found out that they had very ambivalent feelings about the State of Israel, which still existed. Soon they were going out on dates together, fixing each other up with the roommates of the guys they were dating, and when the year was over they decided to live together, sharing a two-bedroom apartment on West 100th Street with a very nice view of Central Park–if you leaned out the kitchen window.

Alice came from Westchester, from an old German Jewish family. She was a philosophy major and also wrote poetry. In their senior year she met Matt, a medical student, who proposed to her on their sixth date. They got married the summer after the four of them graduated. Debbie, Fran, and Susan were her maids of honor. Matt and Alice hadn't planned on it, but Alice ended up getting pregnant six months later, just when she was settling into her first teaching job, at a middle school in the Bronx. She had Benjamin, Warren, and Stephanie, all within five years. Alice stopped writing, never went back to work, and whenever the four of them got together, she looked exhausted. It was Debbie who said, "You'd think with a doctor for a husband she'd be in better shape." But there was always something wrong with her: allergies, migraines, stomach problems. Her kids were eight, ten, and Benjy had just had his bar mitzvah, when Alice was diagnosed with breast cancer. She had surgery, did chemo and radiation, but the cancer metastasized and she was gone just before Warren's bar mitzvah, which Debbie, Susan and Fran attended, as a team of surrogate mothers.

Debbie was from Chicago. Her parents were Russian immigrants, working class, and her family were all Communists. A brilliant student, she was at Barnard on scholarship and wanted to teach little kids. Right out of Barnard she got a job in an elementary school in Queens. The work was engaging and challenging at first, but grew more and more difficult. She started drinking, smoking pot every night, which they'd all experimented with in college, went through a major depression, was in and out of therapy and on and off medication for years. Twice she was hospitalized, once shortly before Alice was gone. After Alice's funeral Debbie went out for coffee with Fran and Susan. That night on the phone Susan said to Fran, "Being with Deb is like being with a zombie." And Fran said to Susan, "It breaks my heart. Do you remember how funny she used to be?" The two would take turns calling Debbie every few months, and the three of them would get together for lunch, or for tea at the Russian Tea Room. One day Susan called Debbie and got a message that the line had been disconnected. Concerned, she called Debbie's mother, now living in Florida. Mrs.

Solomon told her the sad news, that Debbie had been hospitalized, long term. Susan wanted to visit her. Mrs. Solomon said not to. "Half the time she doesn't recognize anyone."

Susan came from Los Angeles. Her father was an entertainment lawyer, her mother had been a minor actress and later became a noted landscape painter. Susan was the prettiest of the four and the most restless. She dated a different guy every weekend, meaning she spent the night with a different guy every weekend. After they graduated she went for her Masters and got a job teaching anthropology at a junior college on Staten Island. She worked there for a year and then through one of her father's connections she got a tenure-track position at NYU. The others were happy for her, but jealous, and very happy for her when she met Martin, a Jewish Studies professor whom she married two years later. Alice and Fran hoped that Susan would settle down now that she was married, but she hadn't even sent out all her thank you cards when she left Martin, moved back to LA, and got a job through her father representing the authors of screenplays. She stopped returning their calls and letters. One day Fran was sitting in her dentist's office flipping through a gossip magazine she would never have read anywhere else, and came upon a picture of Susan and her new husband, a famous and very handsome music producer, who wasn't Jewish. Their divorce a few years later and her next divorce from another rich handsome gentile husband were front page news in all the tabloids. After her third divorce they didn't read about her for a while. When she resurfaced it was as an active fundraiser for the Republican Party, who represented AIPAC in Congress, made several trips to Israel, and became a strong voice in favor of the Occupation. "What happened to her?" Fran wondered, and finally decided—"If you stretch the meaning of the word—very far—you could still say that she's teaching."

Fran had the most unusual background of them all. She was born in Havana to Sephardi parents who emigrated from Turkey, lost everything in the revolution, and escaped to Miami when Fran was four. She arrived in this country speaking Turkish, Spanish, and Ladino–which Alice, Susan, and Debbie had never heard of.

English came easy to her. She majored in Swahili, her goal being to teach English to the children of immigrants. Of the four of them, Fran was the most dedicated to her studies, the one who went out on the fewest dates, perhaps, they decided, because she came from the most traditional family. Right out of Barnard she got a job teaching in an ESL program in Brooklyn, which she loved.

A year before Alice died the four of them had dinner together for the last time. Alice looked terrible and Fran debated telling them, but it was Alice herself who said, "Franny, something is up with you. Tell us." And so it was that she announced to the others that she was a lesbian and had met a wonderful woman at work, who was a Puerto Rican poet who taught sign language. They told her how happy they were for her, that they were looking forward to meeting Olivia. But that night there were back and forth phone conversations between Alice, Susan, and Debbie. "Did you know? Did you suspect?" Alice admitted that she felt happy for her, and sad that Fran had not shared this important piece of her life with them. Debbie was delighted–she'd been worried about Fran being alone, finally understood why, and hoped she'd be happy. Susan didn't say so but felt uncomfortable, wondering if Fran had ever been interested in her. And on the way home Fran thought, subway rattling its way back to Brooklyn Heights, "All four of us have gone to hell, but I think I'm the only one who's coming back."

A year later, right after Alice's funeral, Fran and Olivia bought a fixer-upper brownstone in Park Slope. Nico was born a year after that. Fran was his birth mom–his donor was Olivia's brother Jose. Three years later she gave birth to Alicia, named for their friend, and two years after that Fran gave birth to Devorah, for Debbie who was hospitalized for what turned out to be the rest of her life. Fran eventually became the principal of the school where they taught. Olivia's first book of poetry was widely acclaimed, her second won a Pulitzer, and from their agreement to raise the kids Jewish, Olivia eventually converted.

Fran and Olivia were happy that their kids had bonded with Alice's kids, from years of sharing holidays and other special events with them. And when the kids were all out of the house, Olivia and Fran decided that it was time for a joint career switch. They both went off to rabbinic school, were ordained at the same time, and now share a pulpit at an LGBTQ synagogue in San Francisco. They did all the work on their second fixer-upper, an old wood-frame house in Bernal Heights, and since living there their book of women's commentaries on the Torah, their second book about celebrating Jewish holidays, and their most recent book, *To Hell and Back: A Family Guide to Spiritual Practice* have all become best sellers, translated into Hebrew, Arabic, Greek, French, Spanish, Russian, Portuguese, Yiddish–and Ladino!–with a video version in American Sign Language due out next year, with Spanish and Hebrew signed versions to follow.

Fragment 1

[...]
    . . . Rabbi Sara-Rosa said, "We are told in the Shema to love YHWH our God with all our heart and all our soul and all our might. But when are we permitted to be angry at It, to hate It?'"

Rabbi Shulawitz said, "Whenever we feel those feelings."

Hazzan Costello said, "Always."

Rabbi Yitzchak said, "Never?"

Rabbi Manashe said, "Transmute it."

Hazzanit Abbas inquired, "Did you mean transmute *it*–the feelings, or *It*–God?"

Rabbi Meller said, "God. Goddess. Goddix."

Kohenet Sidona said, "I find myself thinking of the number of times in the "Amidah" when we speak of God as the One who gives life to the dead, and I'm hoping, in an almost Christian way, that those words aren't just a statement of fact but a prophecy, because otherwise [...]

Celebrating the Seven Days
of Shavuot

by Rabbi Ella bat Levi Morgan from
Kyoto, Japan

In the Torah our ancestors were instructed to make three annual pilgrimages to the temple in Jerusalem–at Sukkot, Passover,
and Shavuot. Both Sukkot and Passover are weeklong celebrations,
noted for their joyous observances, but Shavuot has long been a
one or two day festival with few symbolic rituals. While its origins
are agricultural–Shavuot was the season when the first fruits and
grains were brought to the temple–over time it's come to be observed as the anniversary of the giving of the Torah at Sinai.

Shavuot, which means "Weeks" in Hebrew, occurs seven
weeks and one day after Passover. In the old days, in many different communities, the synagogue was decorated with plants and
flowers, and the agricultural roots of the festival are still recalled
by eating dairy meals, whenever possible. *The Book of Ruth*, with
its harvest references and woman-to-woman love, is always read
on Shavuot.

Some communities stay up all night studying from the Tanach and rabbinic texts. This custom began in mystical circles in
16th century Safed as a way of preparing Jews to receive the Torah
once again. Expanding on this tradition, in a time of fear when
the need for community is greater than ever, I propose that we
extend our Shavuot observance to a full week, dedicating each day

to another level of Torah study, using Torah in the broadest sense. Texts will be chosen each year to expand upon our understanding of revelation and deepen our capacity to be vessels of Divine Inspiration. Study sessions can incorporate music by Jewish composers, art by Jewish artists, along with meditation and movement, from dancing to dance midrash. During these sessions we will also create stories, prayers, poems, songs, dances, and images that emerge from our studies, and that will support the work of radical healing and transformation on our planet.

The First Day of Shavuot–will be organized around texts and themes from the Tanach.

The Second Day of Shavuot–will be organized around texts and themes from the Talmud.

The Third Day of Shavuot–will be organized around texts and themes from Midrash.

The Fourth Day of Shavuot–will be organized around texts and themes from Kabbalah and from Jewish mystical texts.

The Fifth Day of Shavuot–will be organized around texts and themes from our siddurim and machzorim.

The Sixth Day of Shavuot–will be organized around Jewish writings from ancient and medieval times until the beginning of the Enlightenment.

The Seventh Day of Shavuot–the final day of this holiday will be organized around texts written by Jewish writers in the centuries since the Enlightenment, in all genres, secular and religious, from every Jewish community in the world, including novels, stories, poems, prayers, essays, films, etc.

A 23rd Psalm

BY HAZZAN ANITA SCHWARTZ-D'ESPAÑA
OF NEW TEMPLE ZION, NEW ZEALAND

.

A Psalm of Bathsheba

The Shechinah is my fashion consultant,
I shall not want.
In lush stores She makes me try on things
and to elegant boutiques She guides me.
She restores my soul.
She directs me on the path of bargains
for the sake of Her good taste.

If I should walk through a valley of schmattes
I fear no embarrassment
for You are with me.
Your needle and spool of thread
comfort me.
You prepare a full closet before me
in the face of jealous neighbors.
You wash my head
with fragrant shampoos
till my tub overflows.

Let beauty and kindness enfold me
all the days of my life.
And I shall dwell in the walk-in closet
of the Divine One
forever.

The Bird

BY MAGGID BEATA ROMAN

WHEN I WAS A girl, my mother and I watched the video of the very last bird in the world dying. It was a small gray nondescript creature, its final moments broadcast around the world on the Outernet, including footage of the very moment that it was gone. The bird was in a very large cage in a laboratory at Stanford University, a cage of many levels, large enough for the bird to fly around in, in every direction. When I called it a cage my mother sighed and said, "It's an aviary, dear." But I'd never heard that word before. Never saw one before, either. Or, ever again, except once in a museum.

The video was very long, but we watched the whole thing. Just watching it, it was hard for us to tell when the bird was gone, as it was lying motionless on its side in a nest of straw at the very bottom of the cage for the entire video. The only way that we could tell that it was gone was from watching the monitor at the bottom of screen that was recording its vital signs. There was scarcely anything moving on that monitor the whole time. Perhaps that's a lesson for all of us–that being dead isn't really so different from being alive.

It was, as I said, a small bird, gray and nondescript. But when the line on the monitor stopped and then disappeared, and the narrator, the Brazilian scientist who'd raised the bird in that lab, began to cry, I started to cry myself, and so did my mother, who excused herself and went into her room.

After it was over I phoned my big sister Rachie to ask her if she'd watched. She said no. I told her that I cried. She asked why. I was speechless. She said, "You were always so sentimental. I mean, it's not like you knew the bird, and it's not like any of us have even seen a bird in the wild for the last ten or fifteen years." I hung up on her.

Speaking of Our Forefathers

RECORDED BY RABBI MIRIAM SHABAZI

RABBI SADIE SAID, "ABRAHAM Lincoln was in love with Abraham Jonas, the Jewish lawyer and legislator."

Rabbi Julio said, "There was no love; only friendship."

Rabbi Sadie said, "You can feel it in their letters, written in a very different time."

Rabbi Julio said, "With all due respect, you can imagine anything you want. You are a storyteller, but I am an historian."

Rabbi Hildy stated, "We have the words of the esteemed Rabbi Isaac Meyer Wise, who delivered a eulogy after Lincoln's death in which he stated that Lincoln had told him that he was a descendant of the Hebrew people."

Rabbi Erick said, "Lincoln was speaking figuratively."

Rabbi Sadie said, "He was speaking literally, recalling anecdotes told in his family."

Rabbi Julio said, "There is absolutely no evidence from any source to validate Wise's statement, not then and not since then, and Lincoln's own son Robert later denied Wise's claim."

Rabbi Erick said, "Yes, but isn't it unusual for that time that he had Jewish friends, associates, a Jewish doctor, Jewish supporters, and that he repealed the only directly anti-Semitic bill in all of American history until the 21st century?"

Rabbi Sadie said, "If you review the life of Lincoln you can see again and again that if he wasn't gay, he was certainly bisexual."

Rabbi Julio said, "You just changed the subject. Again."

Rabbi Hildy said, "Isn't it our job to paint a broad portrait of Jewish history, particularly here in what now seems to be our homeland, in a time when as never before in our long history the words 'Next year in Jerusalem' have become an impossibility?"

Rabbi Julio said, "Yes, history. Not historical fiction. And while we can state with certainly that Lincoln was a friend to the Israelites of his time–please remember that the word Jew was seldom used then, due to its negative connotations–there is absolutely no historical evidence for his homosexuality–or for his Hebraic ancestry."

Rabbi Erick said, "I was standing on a street corner once, on the way home from school when one of my classmates was hit by a car. Fortunately, he was fine. When the police arrived and questioned us, each one of us who'd seen the car hit Jason told a different story about what had happened."

Rabbi Sadie said, "History is told by the victors."

Rabbi Julio said, "It may be told by the victors, but it's written by trained historians."

Rabbi Hildy said, "From Abraham our father to Abraham Lincoln, there was none like Abraham."

This is What I Want to Hear

by Rabbi Trish McCohen of Congregation Bnai Shalom in Edinburgh, Scotland

Don't tell me about the Shechinah.
How God's female aspect
is a sacred part of our tradition.
The word "aspect" gives it all away.

Your Shechinah is God's sidekick
chum
Supergirl to Superman
a Purim drag costume.
She's His sad dark girlfriend
evicted from her Jerusalem apartment
by the Romans
and wandering ever since.

I don't want an Aspect in my prayers
not even that upgrade to First Class
Yah Shechinah.
Yah is a masculine form
not the Tah Shechinah that would
make it truly female.

This is what I want
and nothing less
if we really mean
that God isn't Male.
I want prayers to Her
that don't frighten us into thinking
"This is paganism. Heresy.
Something we've avoided for
two thousand years!"
I want Her presence to be felt
Her names to be called
Her blessings to be known
Just as His are.

I want:
May She who makes peace
in Her high heavens.
I want:
And on the seventh day She rested.
I want:
Holy Holy Holy
is the Lady of Hosts
the whole earth is full of Her glory.

I want new liturgy to Her
or I want us to throw out
everything stale and male and old.
I want generations of Jewish girls
and boys
to grow up hearing us pray to Her.
Creator
Sustainer
Queen of Heaven
Mother of all.

I want us to bask in Her magnificence.
Her glory.
I want us to midrash Miriam
in the cleft of lightning-struck tree
as She flashes by
shining.
I want the cosmos to be Her challah
shaped and molded.
The universe Her handiwork.
Her offspring
birthed from Her Sacred Self
and never separate from It.

Is this too much to ask
of a tradition that has reinvented itself
over and over again
for three thousand years?
Not contracted fear
but expansion and open embrace.
Reverence.
Recognition.
That we see in Her
what we find in ourselves
and see mirrored in ourselves
what we find in Her:
One
Eternal
Ever-present
Creator of the Universe
Source of Life.
Our Mother
Our Comfort
Our God/dess.

The Dog

by Maggid Beata Roman

SUNLIGHT WAS STREAMING THROUGH the window, its long arms caressing the large dun-colored dog that was lying fast asleep on the Persian carpet beside the living room couch, the carpet red and yellow and bought second-hand at a garage sale. The dog a dull tan, long and nondescript. The dog was old but not too old, for a large dog of its noble variety, with an expected lifespan promising it two or three more good years, 'good years' being a euphemism for 'period of reasonable canine activity.' The fact that it was somewhat deaf seemed to bother neither itself nor its person, who in fact was glad to no longer be startled in the middle of the night by said dog leaping into awakeness whenever a police car or fire truck came though their otherwise quiet neighborhood, sirens wailing.

The person attached to the dog was sitting on the couch with its breathing mask on, as it had just come in from work at the institution of higher learning, a noted yeshiva, where it served as an instructor in the at-times maligned subject of theology. Once, upon walking down the hallway from the elevator, the dog would have raced to the door and begun to bray, but those days were over, to the person's joy–and sorrow. It liked being welcomed home by braying and nails scratching on the other side of the door by a large dog standing on its hind legs, who would dart around the opening door and leap up at its person's chest, paws digging into its jacket, slobbering love all over its face in welcome. But today, as most days, the dog looked up from its cozy place in the sun,

sun too fierce to go outdoors without covering, but comforting on chilly autumn days when its rays are filtered through layers of glass. Yes, today as most days, the dog–let us call her Cordelia, for that is what the person named it–today as most days Cordelia looked up at the person–let us call him Geoffrey, for that is what his single mother Leonora named him–Geoffrey whose Hebrew name is Gershom, came in to see Cordelia lift up her shaggy head, give him the dog equivalent of a smile, and then go back to sleep.

Watching Cordelia sleep, Geoffrey slowly took off his gloves, then his breathing mask, and put them down on the coffee table. He reached down and scratched Cordelia behind her floppy left ear, which caused her to open her eyes for a moment, smile at him again, and then fall right back to sleep. Cordelia had always been a prodigious dreamer, ever since he'd first brought her home from the pound when she was small enough to fit in his cupped hands. Sound asleep she would bray and bark and growl and whimper, and her legs would quiver and dart, so that he could usually tell what she was dreaming–hunting, fetching, mating, or playing–laying almost always on her side, but every once in a while flat on her back, her legs comically up in the air, scurrying, racing.

Those dreams of hers–were ancient. They went back more than forty thousand years, back to the years when dogs were first being domesticated–or, were they actually domesticating?–actually training a whole other species to provide food, shelter, companionship and comfort for them, grooming and caring and providing an assured place for their young to be cared for as well, in exchange for a few short hours of work and a regular supply of expressed gratitude. Yes, those dreams of hers were ancient, going back even further, all the way back to the years when her ancestors were still wild, still wolves, still a part of the unified fabric of nature.

In her dreams Cordelia was still a part of nature, although she herself had only been out of doors twice in her entire life, once on the way to the pound and once again on her way to Geoffrey's apartment. Being out of doors is now dangerous for all life forms. That I do not have to tell you. And yes, there is a company that makes breathing masks for dogs–but without exception they find them too uncomfortable to wear for more than a few moments before they try to claw them off. Sadly, all the stray outdoor dogs in the world have perished. The rest live sheltered if constrained lives indoors. But we know that when asleep, dogs enter a time-less world where there are still birds to leap up at and squirrels to race after, on lawns that vanished–long ago. And blessedly–or is it a curse?–for a moment or two, watching Cordelia's large dunny paws scurrying, Geoffrey is able to forget that himself, and scurry after her.

Lecha Dodi

by Rabbi Omar Elias of
the Temple Eden Kweer Minyan,
Oakland, California

Buck Abramowitz
six four
two o eight
not mystical numbers
just height, weight
with shoulders like lumberjack
and, since April
on the far side of forty, a Taurus
stands in a low-cut
strapless
black velvet
evening gown
beefy calf length
barefoot
his size thirteens
clutching the hard wood floor

thick wavy black hair
shot with gray
four days unshaven

goatee
that grows south
into forest of black fur
curling up and around
his tight fitting dress
bought thrift
flexing his pecs
not to show off
but from nervousness
this his first time in drag

"You're a natural,"
says boyfriend
José Rosenbaum
Argentinean great great grandchild
of Holocaust survivors
now downstairs in the men's room
taking a leak
before services begin
José, raised Orthodox
this Buck's first time
in shul
since his bar mitzvah
still then short and thin
Reform suburban Chicago
Grandma Sophie kvelling

and the tiny glass beads
sewn by hand around the neckline
catch the light
as Buck shifts in the doorway
this Purim night
also the beginning of Shabbat
waiting for José

thinking
"How the hell
did I ever let him talk me into this?"

José returns
oblivious
to what's going on
around him
checks the front
of his white tuxedo pants
to make sure he's zipped
then slips his arm
up though Buck's
and leads him into the sanctuary
just as everyone stands
and turns toward the door

and the lights
catch rhinestones in the tiara in
Baruch Abramowitz's wavy black hair
shot with gray
and bounce off the beads
sewn by hand
by Carmela Rodriguez
fifty years before
when she made this dress
to wear
at her sister Estrellita's wedding

Notes for: **Lecha Dodi**

Place: at the doors to a sanctuary
Time: Purim, the festival that celebrates the survival of the
Jews in ancient Persia, story told in the Bible in the book of Esther.

Lecha Dodi: means, "Come my beloved." This prayer is said on Friday evening to welcome in the Sabbath. It's the newest major addition to the Jewish liturgy, only dating back to the Safed Kabbalists of 16th century, who would go out in the fields in white robes to welcome in the Sabbath Queen with the words, "Come, O Bride."

Buck–think of buck-naked, think of "stately plump Buck Mulligan" in Joyce's *Ulysses*, Jewish Leopold Bloom's friend. Also a reference to the horned animals, stags and gazelles, that are used as symbols of male sexuality in "Song of Songs" and other Jewish erotic poems, including those to same-sex lovers written by medieval Spanish rabbis.

Abramowitz–means Son of Abraham, in Jewish Russian, Anglicized.

lumberjack–think of trees and the Tree of Life when you read this word, and think about the sacred posts dedicated to the goddess Asherah, that the Tanach so frowns upon.

a Taurus–the astrological sign of the bull, perhaps an allusion to the golden calf.

strapless black velvet evening gown–cross-dressing is forbidden in the Torah, but on Purim, when this poem takes places, one is encouraged to drink to excess, and there is some flexibility about what's prohibited and what's permitted.

barefoot–like Moses at the burning bush.

forest of black fur–again, think trees and wild animals, sex, love, "Song of Songs."

José–Joseph, Yosef in Hebrew, means, "He shall add," just as he and Buck are adding to our tradition. We are told in the Torah that Joseph was beautiful.

Rosenbaum–from the roses (probably better translated as lilies or lotuses) in "Song of Songs," means Rosetree, again the Tree of Life.

Grandma Sophie–from "Sophia," the goddess of Wisdom in Gnostic texts and Jewish Wisdom literature, mentioned in the book of *Proverbs*.

kvelling–Yiddish, "bursting with pride," usually it's parents and grandparents who kvell, over the accomplishments of their offspring.

white tuxedo pants–Buck is in black, José is in white. Think marriage, think yin and yang, union of male and female, with the ambiguity of big butch Buck in drag and shorter José in a white tuxedo. We know he's short because he slips his arm up through Buck's.

zipped–or maybe not. Think of his genitals, think of his sexuality, think of his love for Buck in his tight black dress, a dress that José had to alter so that Buck could fit in it.

stands and turns toward the door–this is what the congregation does when they sing the last verse of Lecha Dodi.

rhinestone tiara–the high priest's miter, maybe Moses's mistranslated "horns."

Baruch–Buck's Hebrew name, Baruch, means "Blessed," and also refers to the blessing that comes from his and José's relationship. His English name is probably Barry.

Carmela–from the word for a garden in Hebrew. Think of Mount Carmel and Elijah the prophet.

Estrellita–a Spanish form of Esther, the savior of her people and the hero of Purim, her name comes from the Babylonian goddess of love, Ishtar. And think of weddings, unions, sacred marriages, of two men, of God and the Sabbath. Two sisters, two men.

Blessings from the Genizah of Dreams

By Rabbi Danit Doron of the Synagogue
of Exiles, Madrid

And God said to Sarah, "Sarale, I will make your offspring as numerous as the stars in the sky. They will spread out across the earth and inhabit every continent, every nation, every city, from Kaifeng in China to Brooklyn in New York. And they will do wonderful things, and they will also suffer a great deal, as will any people that survives for a very long time. And because you laughed at me when I told you at age 99 that you were going to have a child–which was a sane response for any post-menopausal woman–down through time, all of your descendants will have great senses of humor, and wherever they dwell they shall make other people laugh, in the stories they write, the comedy acts they perform, and in the movies and on television, two future inventions that they will contribute to in many significant ways."

"And please listen," God said to Jacob, his little Yankele, "I will make your descendants as numerous as the stars, as uncountable as the grains of sand on a beach. And although you have been a liar and a cheat, a little too smart sometimes for your own good, all of your descendants will be smart too, but not so good at sports. And I will send them to every part of the world. Remember that, every part of the world. I don't want them to stay in one place.

And wherever they go, wherever they stop and rest for a while, anywhere in the world, that place will be called after you, Eretz Macholel, the land of the people who dance with God. And in every place that they stop shall be heard the sounds of music. And the earth will tremble from the rhythm of their dancing feet, and the air will resound with their songs of joy and the clapping of their upraised hands."

Reframing the Festival of Dedication for Our Time

BY RABBI ELIEZER ELIZABETH O'CONNOR
OF SYDNEY, AUSTRALIA

HOW SHOULD WE CELEBRATE Hanukkah, the Festival of Dedication?

Our dear colleague Rabbi Ilura Hadasi said that in the Karaite tradition we should not celebrate it at all.

Hazzan Toby Minsk said, "In times such as these, we should not celebrate it at all because its roots are in division and in war and we who remain are required to create a world of unity and of peace."

Rabbi Marc Romanelli said, "I remember as a boy when there were still wax candles, before the use of fossil fuels was outlawed."

Professor Carmina Rabinovitch said, "And I remember when there were still beeswax candles. Before the last of the bees became extinct."

Hazzan Shira FitzJacob said, "My grandmother was a big environmentalist and she always used to burn them."

Rabbi Jacob Ovadia wrote in his book, *Undoing the Past In Order to Create the Future:* "For many many centuries we have followed the teachings of the House of Hillel that require us to illuminate one light on the first night and add a light on each succeeding night. But in this time of increasing darkness I propose that we revert to the teachings of the House of Shammai and begin the first night of Hanukkah with all eight lights lit and remove one each night to mark our passage into increasing darkness."

Inspired by his teachings, Maggid Naftalia DaSilva suggested the following ritual:

On the first night we light all eight lights and say–"This is the promise of our illuminated world in all its holy fullness."

On the second night we only light seven lights and say–"Now there is no clean air, because of what we have done to the Earth."

On the third night we only light six lights and say–"Now there is no clean water, because of what we have done to the Earth."

On the fourth night we only light five lights and say–"Now the trees and plants are dying, because of what we have done to the Earth."

On the fifth night we only light four lights and say–"Now the insects, the birds of the air, the fish of the seas, and the animals of the land are all dying, because of what we have done to the Earth."

On the sixth night we only light three lights and say–"Now communities are dying, cities are dying, nations are dying, people are dying everywhere from things that never killed before, from plagues and scourges that our ancestors could not have imagined, because of what we have done to God's holy Earth."

On the seventh night we only light two lights and say–"Now we stand here, but tomorrow we might be gone from God's holy Earth."

On the eighth and last night we only light one single light and then we shall say–"Now only hope remains, hope which is our call to action. And it is to this that we must dedicate ourselves for this festival night and for all of the days that remain to us on God's holy damaged Earth."

Rabbi Malkah bat Tuvia said, "The memory of what was, yes. Observance, yes. And words of blessing, yes. But in our world of scarcity and poverty and much too much heat–I believe that we should burn no lights at all, nor any kind of bulbs or candles, not on this holiday or even on Shabbat. I believe that we should set out on our tables only empty candlesticks. No lights at all but those we conjure in our hearts. Remembering the primal light of creation rather than those lights of our own flawed making."

Fragment 2

[...]

Concerning the nature of good and bad, as reflected in Torah and in our own lived experiences, Professor Ripley-Kahn from Hebrew Union College, Juneau, Alaska, said, "I find it helpful in every moment of decision to imagine that I myself am our mother Eve, standing alone in the Garden of Eden."

Hazzanit Beruriah Yakoub of Tunis said, "We're told in *Isaiah 45:7* that God forms light and creates darkness, makes shalom–wholeness, peace–and creates bad. I struggle with this, wanting there to be only peace in the world. But when I look out at the cosmos, at comets smashing into planets and stars going nova–I realize that what seems so awful around me done by humanity–is part of the universe itself."

Professor Ilana Merkaz said, "We saw what happened, in a world where 80% of violent crimes are committed by men, in cities where from pre-school on athletic competition was entirely replaced by dance and music classes. Those cities saw a 68.7% drop in crime, and a flowering of dance and music and allied arts that cannot be measured by statistics."

[...] and on the brink of total extermination, perhaps our sacred texts have led us astray. Or, perhaps we have not read them right, or read them well, or [...]

[...] the two most destructive inventions of the last two centuries, we unanimously agreed in our last session–were the atomic bomb–and wireless technology. Each of them, we agreed, were destructive in three ways–the atomic bomb for shattering the coherent energy-field of the planet, for damaging it physically, and unlike conventional bombs, for continuing to damage the planet over long stretches of time. And wireless technology for damaging our DNA, for causing damage to the neural pathways of our brains, and also for shattering the coherent social fabric of our connections with each other. The first [. . .] but the second, on a more [. . .] because of what we were taught about not placing a stumbling block before the blind, and thus we [. . .]

Carol Flightworthy the maggid of Woodstock said, "There is little in our texts that comforts or guides me. I find it more useful to remember the wisdom of those Native Americans who taught us to remember that any decision we make will affect the next seven generations and then I [. . .] "

[. . .] long gone themselves and [. . .]

[. . .] probably don't have that long to [. . .]

In the Garden of Eating

by Anita Gilman, the Great Maggidah
of all Canada

Goddix planted a garden in Eden and put there the man It had formed.

The woman It had formed.

The singular person It had just formed in Its own image.

And Goddix said to the woman:

Goddix said to the man:

Goddix said to the person:

"Of every tree in the garden you are free to eat; but if you eat the fruit on the tree of death, you will surely die."

"You will find especially delicious the fruit of the tree of knowledge of good and bad, and I hope that you will eat from it regularly to inspire your embodied adventures."

"As for the tree of enlightenment, you are always welcome to eat from it, but I suspect that its fruits are too high up in the branches for you to often reach."

"And these are the rules, My darlings. Now, go and live."

That Which is Holy

BY RABBI MYRA BERURIAH OF ODESSA, TEXAS

WE BEGAN OUR SESSION by looking at these words:

Kadosh–set apart, consecrated, sacred, holy

Kiddush–the blessing over wine

Kaddish–a prayer, the version of which for mourners, is the most familiar

Kedushah–a section of the Amidah

Kiddushin–a wedding, ring ceremony

Kadesh/Kadeshah–a male/female sacred prostitute

Mikdash–a holy place, a temple

Then we explored these texts:

God called to him out of the bush: "Moses! Moses!" He answered, "Here I am." And God said, "Don't come closer! Remove your sandals from your feet, for the place on which you stand is holy ground." Ex. 3:4–5

You shall be to Me a kingdom of priests and a holy nation. Ex. 19:6

Remember the Sabbath day and keep it holy. Ex. 20:8

You shall be holy, for I, the Eternal your God, am holy. Lev. 19:2

You shall sanctify yourselves and be holy, for I the Eternal am your God. You shall faithfully observe My laws. I the Eternal make you holy. Lev. 20:7–8

The questions the ten of us asked yesterday in our four-hour session all ripple out from those texts and those words. We asked and have no answers for this question–"What is holy in a time when the world appears to be dying? What can we do, say, pray, in such a time? How can we remember our mission when we are under attack on every front and frequently blamed for the entire situation we find ourselves in?"

Rabbi Maltz of Cleveland said, "Nothing is different now than it was in the past."

Rabbi Abouav of Pretoria said, "The hour is late, the call is urgent, the doctor is all of us, there is no time to wait."

Maggid Peretz of Hong Kong said, "We watched our islands vanish beneath a rising sea. We are like Noah and his wife, unnamed in Torah and called Naamah in rabbinic texts, they and their children and all of us in exile from the familiar. We know what to do. Be holy protectors of whatever survives. Else we too will go nameless. Faceless. Lifeless."

Hazzan Sclama of Havana said, "If not now–is a little too late."

Rabbah Davidi of Prague said, "The ground is still holy, and nearly everything we had and held dear has been removed from us."

Rabbi Ibrahima-Weiss of Managua said, "Everything is holy, even when we set ourselves apart from it by our thoughts, our feelings, and our actions."

Rabbi Tenur of Montréal said, "We cry out like Job. But there seems to be no hope of renewal. Has the One who sometimes turns Its back on us done so? We cry out in the night but there is no answer."

Rabbi Meller-Watanabe of San Juan said, "In this hour, hope is the first child of Bathsheba and David, the one who died before Solomon was born."

Rabbi de Beautmont-Kahn-Greenberg of Winnipeg said nothing.

Elegance

BY MAGGID BEATA ROMAN

THIS IS THE MOST elegant sight in the world, to me–a man, somewhat older and handsomely dressed, walking down the street on a
late fall morning–carrying in his hands a pair of gloves. They can be
knit gloves, although leather, thin and dark, has its own particular
appeal. Where that image comes from–my early childhood. From
no one in particular and from every somewhat older man I ever
saw, wearing a long overcoat, walking with a purposeful stride,
those two gloves pressed together, even perhaps slightly rolled up
over themselves in his cool palm. Or, he is paused, poised, perhaps
at a doorway, having just rung the bell and now waiting to be admitted. He might be a friend, a parent, a doctor, a gentleman caller.
He might be canvassing for an election, he might be wearing a hat,
or not. But that image, of his hands, his large sleek hands, clutching
those mirror-image gloves, is to me not just the most elegant sight
in the world–but a sight almost holy.

Remember how it was. When we could expose our skin outside, even on the coldest days. Remember how it was to lie out
on the grass, in shorts and a tee shirt. Remember how it was to
lie naked, or almost naked, on a beach almost anywhere in the
world, the sun caressing your skin like a lover. I know, I know,
billions of you are too young to remember that. You are too young
to remember so many wonderful things, like breathing in the air
directly, as you walk down a city street, a pair of kid gloves in your
swinging hands. Too young to remember what I really mean when

I say–cold days. Too young to know anything but heat, heat and more heat.

My air-fix is on snuggly, my gloves are sealed to my jacket, my jacket is firmly attached to my pants, which slip under my shoes so that no part of me is exposed to the toxic air of any overly hot day anywhere on Planet Earth. Perhaps I am elegant, perhaps I am beautiful. Once upon a time, people on warm days all over the planet walked the streets of towns and cities free from all encumbrances. We walked the streets of the world, wandered in parks, along the ocean, barefoot, shirtless, in shorts, in skirts long and skirts short, covered and uncovered and free to do either.

And all of that I long for, still dream about, for almost all of my dreams are about the past now. But oddly, when my heart is breaking, breaking from the state of the world, the image that most clearly comes to me is–yes, I realize it now–it is my great grandfather, Max, walking down Flatbush Avenue with me, my little legs trying to keep up with his long stride, my long skirt flapping around my bare scrawny legs. He has a hat on, but the day is warming up, his tan overcoat is unbuttoned, and he's taken his gloves off. They are gently resting in his long right hand, dark black leather. We stop at a corner, waiting for the traffic light to turn green. (For there were lights then, not directions on when to stop and start delivered to your implant.) He leans down to smile at me, reaches out his bare left hand and rumples my hair. And those gloves, the warm smell of them right in front of me, that vision, that memory, image, far more than any visions of angels, is what conjures up heaven on earth for me now. Two gloves, and two bare hands. Heaven–the impossible.

The Shechinah

by Rabbi Ruby Fernweiss

She walked into the room
unannounced
as was her pretense.
everyone knew she'd been
invited.
Word of the guest list
had been leaked
by the hostess's maid
a month before the party.
That was why everyone
accepted the invitation.
The host, of course
was surprised and pleased
that people who had snubbed him
in the past, all accepted.
He planned an elaborate
feast, and had to call in
extra servants.
There was to be a concert,
a dance piece, and then
a buffet meal.

She arrived
alone
at ten past ten.
Some, naturally, turned her way,
bowed and even scraped.
Some nodded, while others in fact,
the majority, in order
to show how calm, wise
oblivious or unimpressed
they were
by her serene, her imperial
in fact by her divine presence
turned their backs or walked away.

Later, they all asked each other
if they'd seen her,
and everyone nodded yes,
describing her deep blue gown
as pink or green or red.

Vidui for Our Collective Guilt

BY RABBI CARLA REISS OF
CONGREGATION BET DEVORAH, BUENOS AIRES

OUR GOD AND GOD of our ancestors, although we did not invent environmental destruction, sexism, homophobia, or religious intolerance, words from our most sacred text have been used for more than two thousand years by our people and others to justify these great wrongs. And now we must ask for forgiveness.

For the way the creation story and its words, "to fill the earth and subdue it" have been used by our people and others to destroy the planet You created and called good, we atone.

For the way the story of Adam and Eve has been used to insure that women's domination by men be seen as divinely ordained, we now atone.

For the way that words in *Leviticus* have been used by our people and others to damage and destroy the lives of men who love men, and by extension all queer people, by making these crimes against humanity seem to be Your will, we must now atone.

For the way that the Torah repeatedly condemns the faiths of other peoples, which has added to the tension in the world, and been used around the planet to divide, vilify, torture, and kill those from other faith traditions, we must surely now atone.

But atonement is not enough. We vow to rectify all wrongs done by us in Your name, individually and collectively, spiritually and legally, so that we live together in peace and wholeness, sharing the Earth's diminished bounty. We vow to create a global society in which all loving hearts, minds, and bodies, made in Your image, find their sacred paths and places in Your holy world.

And let us say: Amen.

Alternate Realities

Professor Natalie Kleinfeld Tutu,
Johannesburg Shul Association

We discussed in our session yesterday the ways in which our most sacred texts have at times supported the imbalances and inequities we find in the world around us. As an example of what might have been possible, Maggid Lydia Rossi read us the standard version of a passage from *Ruth* and then a tiny fragment found by a team of archaeologists in a cave half a mile south of Qumran, a few months before the final evacuation of the Middle East. The fragment was discovered in a clay jar which has been dated to middle Second Temple period.

Ruth 4:16
Naomi took the child and held him to her bosom. She became his foster mother, and the women neighbors gave him a name, saying, "A son is born to Naomi!" They named him Obed; he was the father of Jesse, father of David.

Text from Cave Q3A
[. . .] the child and held him to her bosom. She became his foster mother, and the women neighbors gave him a name, saying, "A son is born to Naomi!" They named him Obed. Then Ruth gave birth to a daughter. She named her Tamar and said, "Now I give a

daughter to Naomi." Obed was the father of Jesse, father of David, and Tamar was the mother of [. . .]

Rabbi Avi de Ville invited us to think of the entire *Torah* as midrash itself–the story of the Garden of Eden a retelling of older stories in which the serpent was sacred to Asherah, not phallic but umbilical. The Tower of Babel–a verbal midrash on Mesopotamian ziggurats. The story of Noah and the flood–our ancestors retelling and reinterpreting the older stories of Utnapishtim and Gilgamesh found on cuneiform tablets.

Professor Leora Abu Levi spoke to us about the stele fragments discovered in Beersheba three years before the final evacuation. The basalt stele has text carved into it in Proto-Hebraic letters, text that clearly predates the verses in *Leviticus 18:22* and *20:13* that have long been interpreted as condemning male homosexuality. Abu Levi, who directed the dig in which the stele fragments were discovered, indicated that the texts that have come down to us in *Leviticus* were most likely later priestly prohibitions on anything that might conflict with their own monopoly on cultic practices.

From the Beersheba Stele
. . . and if a man lies with a male as with a woman, the two shall be considered holy in their town, and the townspeople shall house them for life and go to them for blessings on the new moon.

Rabbi Ava-Mae de Leon read us a very short midrash of hers, one that brought us back to the heart of our conversation on texts, the history of texts, and the meaning of texts, sacred and otherwise:

Hillel's wife Sarah taught that "Eve invented writing after the Expulsion, carving symbols on rocks as she and her husband wandered east from Eden." Shammai's wife Hannah said, "No, it was Naamah the wife of Noah who first invented writing, scratching symbols on animal skins that she prepared after they were sacrificed, using ink she made herself, mixed together from ashes and her tears."

We discussed this midrash with delight and agreed that in our next session we will continue to discuss what it means to encounter Torah not as a primary text or even as a layered and edited version of earlier primary texts but as a work of midrash itself.

Early October at Home

BY TOBIAS THE MAGGID OF THE SUBWAYS

REBECCA WAS SITTING AT the kitchen table doing her homework. Her cat Wing was curled up in her lap, asleep. Rebecca's mother Selda had just gotten home from work and was emptying the dish-laser, about to start their dinner.

"Mommy, I know why all those old people have ugly droopy tattoos, but why do so many of them have holes in their ears and their lips and through their eyebrows?" nine year old Rebecca Ilanabeth Goldberg-Shirazi/Rivera-Heimowitz asked her mother. "Sally says it's because they used to go outside in the bad air without air-fixs on, or body-suits, and their skin started to rot."

Selda laughed. "No, Honey. Back in the old days people used to get their bodies pierced, but the metal rings and posts they put in the holes got in the way of their body-suits and air-fixes, and interfered with their implants."

"Grack! People really did that?"

"Yes. Grandma Susan had piercings in her ears, but she had plastic surgery. Some people like to keep their holes."

"Grandma was pierced?"

"Yes. And so was my cousin Tiffany."

"Glagg!"

"What are you working on, Honey?" Selda asked her daughter, as she put away the last of the dishes.

"North American history."

"Are you listening to music on your implant?"

"No." Pause. "Yes."

"How many times have I told you that you can't do your homework and listen to music at the same time? Turn it off."

"Mom, don't start guzzing me. *You* can't study and listen to music at the same time, but *I* can."

Having gone through this before, Selda turned and walked over to the freezette. A residence technician who installs and repairs home air-locks, she had an emergency call that day from a family whose lock was malfunctioning. Their unit only had one door so they couldn't get out till she repaired it, and it took her all morning just to find the problem. Now she was exhausted, hungry, and didn't want to get into a fight with her daughter. Opening the freezette door, she laughed to herself, remembering her mother's words to her in similar situations. "I hope someday you have a child as difficult as you are!"

The former United States and Canada are now divided into how many countries?
a–three
b–five
c–seven
d–nine

Rebecca Ilanabeth Goldberg-Shirazi /Rivera-Heimowitz thought in her answer, c, on her compu-text and scrolled to the next page, thinking how weird it was that there hadn't always been a Transpacifica, the country she was born in. Wing stirred in her lap and she reached down to scratch him behind the ears for a while. That was his favorite spot, and he began to purr, loudly.

Her back to Rebecca, Selda was staring at a stack of cartons of pre-prepared vacuum-packed meals in the freezette, wondering what she should make. They'd had Mexican the night before, Kirghiz the night before that.

"Mommy, what was it like to go outside without an air-fix on, or a body-suit?"

Selda paused for a moment, her hand on the freezette door. "It's hard to remember. I was so little when we had to start wearing them. And they were all so ugly. The first ones looked like lab technicians' uniforms. Now there are designer styles. You're so lucky. But why don't you ask Grandma about it? She can tell you better than I can. And if you go through her photograph albums you can see lots of pictures of people outside who aren't wearing them."

"I've looked at her albums, but they're all crumbly, and her pictures are so boring. They're all 2-D and flat. But what about my air-fix? Do you think I'm getting too old to have one with Minnie Mouse all over it?"

"I like that fix. And it still fits. Didn't I get it for you for your last birthday?"

"But could you really open the windows in your house, or lay out on the grass in just your inside clothes? With nothing on top of them and nothing to filter the air?"

"Yes. But that was a long time ago, when there was better air and less radiation. Now get back to your homework. Dinner will be ready soon."

Wing was circling in Rebecca's lap, restless. She picked him up and put him on the floor, where he began to rub against her legs for a while, and then wandered off.

New Mexico and what other states in what used to be the United States of America are now parts of Mexicana?

a–Arizona

b–Maine

c–Texas

d–Alabama

e–Louisiana

Selda decided on sushi and noodles and took out two vac-pacs. Rebecca turned around in her chair and said, "Mommy, I forgot to tell you the really diffy news. There's this new boy in my class named Dick–and he has a father."

Selda put the cartons on the counter and turned to her daughter. "Come on, Rebecca. Everyone has some kind of father. A bio father, a donor father, or a tek father."

"No. This boy has a real father. A father who lives with him! He's the first kid I've ever met in my whole entire life who has one."

Selda was stunned. Rebecca's donor dad lived in The Plains. Rebecca saw him two or three times a year. "A live-in father? When Grandma was your age she told me there were still kids who had them. Then it became illegal for fathers to live with their children. But now that all the men in the world are vaccinated for violence and other rampant male disorders I heard that some women are allowing them back in the house. But it's still illegal, and I didn't know that kind of thing was going on around here." Selda paused for a moment, a troubled look on her face, and asked, "What is this little boy like?"

"He looks normal, Mommy. But I can't tell yet. Sally saw his father the other day and said that he looks normal too."

Somewhat relieved, Selda went back to her preparations, put their dinners in the macrowave, and made a mental note to call Sally's mother after dinner.

Name the capitals of the following countries:
a–Cascadia
b–Transpacifica
c–The Commonwealth of the Plains
d–The New Confederacy
c–The United States of Northeast America
d–The Socialist People's Republic of Vermont

Rebecca answered the next question and then thought on the holovision set that was sitting across from her on the counter. For an instant a miniature 3-d cartoon image flashed over the view-pad.

"Rebecca!"

And flashed off.

New France is composed of which two regions?
a–Florida and Ottawa
b–Florida and Louisiana
c–Louisiana and Quebec

"Mommy, can you take me and Sally to the game next week?"

"Honey, I told you yesterday. I have only five drive-units left this month on my aircar. I need four of them to get to work and go shopping. I can either take you to the game or take you to that dance concert, but I can't do both."

"But Transpacifica is playing Canaan. It's the biggest game of the year."

"You can take the air shuttle from school or call Sally and see if her mother has enough units to take you."

"Is it true that before the World Depression the Jews and Arabs in the Middle East hated each other?"

"Didn't you study that last semester?"

"Yes. But I forgot what happened."

"Well, after the global economy collapsed in 2023, only thirty-seven percent of the people in the world still had jobs. That's when lots of old countries fell apart and new ones started. And somehow after that, lots of things were different. For a while the state of Canaan was one of the richest countries in the world and the Jews and the Arabs all lived together peacefully. Before the evacuation. Your cousin TaMima worked there for a while in a collective factory that made nano-pics. But once and for all, will you go back to your homework!"

The life expectancy of the average human being is now 77.9 years.
True / false

"We saw a really old vid in school last week. It was rad. There was this woman in the kitchen making dinner, and she just turned on the sink–and water came out!"

"That's how it was when I was little. You didn't have to com-tab your expected usage before you got any water."

"But what if you used up your weekly ration?"

"There wasn't any, Sweetheart. You could use as much water as you wanted to."

"You mean it just came pouring out of the faucet? And didn't stop?"

"Till you turned it off yourself."

Rebecca, a bath lover, closed her eyes. Once a year, for her birthday, her mother allowed her to take a bath, by rationing for weeks and weeks in advance. She was picturing herself taking a bath every single morning.

"Mommy, I've been thinking."

"Rebecca Ilanabeth Goldberg-Shirazi/Rivera-Heimowitz, if you finished your day school work I want you to get started on your Hebrew School homework!" Selda snapped at her daughter, then checked their dinners in the macrowave.

"I want to change my name."

"I told you before, when you're sixteen and legal you can do anything you want. Grandma Susan changed her name."

"She did? I didn't know that."

"Yes, your Great Grandma Jennifer named her Shanti when she was born."

"That's a silly name. No wonder she never told me about it. But how do you like this?" Rebecca thought on another tab on her compu-text and lifted it up so that her mother could read it.

BECCA GOLD

"That's very nice, dear. Now go back to your homework!"

"But I'm totally starving. When do we eat?"

Selda, leaning with her back on the counter, looked over her right shoulder to the clock on the macrowave. "Do you think you can wait another twenty-seven point five seconds?"

Fragment 3

[. . .]

Rabbi Hildy Sofer replied, "When Hillel said in *Pirke Avot*, 'If I am not for myself who will be for me? If I am only for myself, what am I? And if not now, when?' he was clearly seeing ahead to our own time and our own situation."

Rabbah Sofie Magnes said, "Yes. 'When' is what we're running out of. We can't change the past and it may be too late to even change the present as it leans into the future."

Hazzan Harry Shimon said, "Yes. We confront our teachings and they seem to me at times inadequate. For years I've kept this line from Rabbi Tarfon in *Pirke Avot* posted above my desk on a now-faded file card: 'It is not your duty to complete the work. Nor are you free to desist from it.' But look at the time we're living in. I'm in my eighties. I could never have imagined as a boy running through Sheep Meadow in Central Park that when I was an old man I would have to wear a breathing mask in order to go outside."

[. . .] we must ponder the irony of how peace came at last to the Middle East. A sad tale of . . . . .

. . . decades of total drought and unlivable scorching heat but . . .

. . . "Yet, the question remains–How did we become Amalek?"

Rabbi Lakshmi Sarfati said, "This is simple. We know the statistics. An abused child will grow up to be an abusive parent. We were abused for almost two thousand . . . . .

Maggid Louise Ramirez Kahn said, "That is all behind us now. We and our Palestinian cousins are all in permanent exile. We cannot look back. We have to stop blaming ourselves and each other. It is imperative that we all look out into the future."

Rabbi Max Amaliah said, "In an apocalyptic sense, self-created and not imposed upon us by the Divine, there may be no future. No 'now.' And no one left to tell the stories of the old whens. But when I look at my granddaughter [. . .] "

Text for a Seder on the Margins

BY CHAZZAN MIKAH KATZWALD RODRIGUEZ

IN THE TRADITIONAL PASSOVER Haggadah that goes back to the time of the creation of our first two Talmuds, we read about the Four Sons–the Wise Son, the Wicked Son, the Simple Son, and the Foolish Son Who Does Not Know How to Ask Questions. For the last one hundred years we have also been able to read about the Four Daughters or simply the Four Children. Tonight, at this Seder, in a time when a great plague is spreading across the face of the Earth and in all of our hearts, when the world is dying because of leaders who have acted like children, and when people like us continue to be vilified and tortured and killed—the woes of the world said to be punishment for our sins—it is time for us to talk about the different Elders of our people, asking ourselves—Which one or ones am I?

The Elders who are isolated, alone, trapped, afraid, hidden, hiding and have no idea of what to do or where to go except to pretend, bury the truth and go on living in the best way possible, passing for something they aren't and living half a life. These are the Elders who believe the things they heard about us, or tried to. Haven't some of us been these Elders at times in our lives, and won't we all perhaps at different times become these Elders again? Let us extend compassion and comfort to them, and let them know that we are here, waiting for them to join us, whenever they're ready to emerge.

The Elders who were seen and could not hide, who were taunted, tortured, abused, destroyed. The tomboy, the sissy, who spoke with a lisp or walked with an un-girlish swagger, the boy who liked skirts and dolls, the girl who liked horses and power tools, the misfit, the in-between child, who was battered and tormented, sent off for shock therapy or conversion therapy. Because these Elders could not "pass," even as children, these Elders sometimes chose Death rather than Pain. Aren't these Elders a part of all of us? Let us hold the memory of them in our loving arms, in the Holy of Holies of our beating hearts.

The Elders who did not know what to do or how to do it, or that it could be done. Sometimes they could pass, and sometimes they could not pass. Sometimes they were alone and sometimes they lived in communities where they were seen and tormented, or seen but tokenized, patronized. Sometimes they lived in such a cozy way that even though they were out, they spoke about "them," not "us," and didn't do anything to make the world a better place for all our people. For different reasons, these Elders stood on the brink of change, but did not take the next step. How often have we heard a cry for help, even our own, but not known what to do? Let us send love to these Elders, clarity and community and certainty.

The Elders who stood up, came out, rose up, alone, with others. Sometimes their journeys began when they were isolated and hiding. And sometimes they lived out their lives, seen because they could not hide, and were taunted and tortured. And sometimes they began by knowing there was work to do but didn't know what it was or how to do it. But one day, with preparation or spontaneously, these Elders stopped and faced their abusers, inner and outer, individual and collective. They are the Elders of Courage. They are the Elders of Change. They are a part of each one of us. Let us honor and celebrate these strong and wise Elders, whose work made possible our sitting here tonight in community.

The Elders who grew up in a time, place, or a family in which telling the truth was honored, and being who they really are was celebrated. Even as children, these Elders stepped out into the world with pride. A sense of wholeness and Self-certainty has been the only way these Elders have known how to live. Some of us have been these Elders, and some of us are the parents and teachers of such Elders, who will grow up wise and loving, strong and tender, until all of us are Elders like these. And these are the Elders who will not pass over, or pass by, but will pass *with* all our people into a better world.

Consecrated Ugliness

BY NAFTALI BEN TSURIS, JEWISH THEOLOGICAL
SEMINARY, BANGKOK

god's mind was elsewhere, the prophet said.
like a man playing cards, or hot on the edge of a
conversation.
when it seems like he's there, but his mind has gone
elsewhere.
only no one can tell us where god's mind went.
it wasn't exactly like he was gone. just part of him.
(and then the world happened.)

trees grow up between cracks in the street
a moment of light appears in the midst of suicidal madness,
and then vanishes,
like sleeping with a hooker,
or being married to a drunk,
some of god is elsewhere.
don't you agree?

it was five o'clock in the morning.
Bathsheba woke, anxiously.
outside the walls she could hear the voices of her husband's
servants
going about their tasks.

a man who loved her
lay with a heavy arm
flopped over her breast.
did anyone ask her?
no.
and now they fight and die for something she does not
care about.

october came and went.
november slapped itself across the faces of all interested
parties.
if a person lived long enough
they could see war/peace/war recirculate
in cynical compulsion.

the priestess offered up the heart of a goat.
on her arms, there were bronze snakes entwined.
she cried out to the great mother.
the clouds sped west. one looked like a bear.
she prophesized victory.
sunset cast its amber glow on the bodies of her sons.

it seems, the lunatic said
that god is on vacation.
in some kind of florida of the mind.
warm. lazy. and sometimes sends a post card.

the priest blesses the wine.
says the right words.
lifts his elegant long-fingered hand
in the proper benediction.
(his mind is on
the thigh of the young woman in the front row
wandering toward her crotch

as he lifts the chalice.)

flowers wilt in an old mayonnaise jar.
a picture taped to the wall
slowly slides in the embrace of gravity.

at her desk, a young woman sits, writing.
the paper is white.
the ink is red,
she thinks of the pain in his last letter
she thinks of the pain and love she used to feel
before there was boredom.

at sunrise, three gulls
attach themselves across the sky.
the light split over the horizon
like too many swords.
the sand was cold.
his bare feet were cold.
he knew that the end was in the heart of the middle.
he felt it.
but nothing was consecrated,
and he wanted to try.
to make love happen.
but the prophet told him
that god was half asleep,
(or is it half awake?)

planets turn.
and crumble.
this is consecrated ugliness.
pain.
sorrow.
heartache.

god raises his voice and says
let there be . . .
but his mind is on things
we will never even be able to dream about.

Good?

BY RABBI RIVKA MALKA O'SHAUGHNESSY

It is good
Ki tov
the Torah says You said
of all that You created.
Good, the rabbis tell us
because You'd made other worlds before
and learned from Your mistakes.

Four homeless people live in doorways on my street.
Wife and baby's corpses washed up bloated, evening news
tells.
My home city has been bombed, cradle of de-civilization.
Houses bulldozed by the army, in retaliation.
At the end, my mother,
her body paralyzed except for her right hand
the nails of which she gnawed again
after sixty years of long and red.

Good? You call this good?
If you are truly God, I say–
You could do better.

The Concert

BY MAGGID BEATA ROMAN

THE TICKETS WERE VERY expensive and sold out immediately. My mother got me a single one through an old friend of hers from graduate school, whose ex-husband's new wife's rabbi sister is on the board of the symphony. The ticket was a return favor for my having given my mother's friend good legal advice when she was getting a divorce from that husband, with whom she remained the best of friends–and not just because they had to be friends in order to co-parent their children. They had none.

My seat was in the first row of the first balcony, a most excellent seat. A couple sat beside me who were jabbering away in sign language. I wished that I knew it. The hall was completely filled. Tickets, my mother's friend told me, were selling on the black market for as much as two thousand dollars. But that's no surprise, when the visiting conductor is from Moscow, and world renowned.

I took off my shoes. And relaxed. The couple beside me–my seat was on the aisle–settled in too. There was silence when the conductor, Natalia Romanovna, entered the stage, crossed it, and ascended the podium. There was silence as she bowed. There was silence as she raised her baton in her left hand, high above that vast empty stage, and there was silence for the next three hours, with no intermission–which I thought would be challenging but was not, due I think to the genius of Romanovna.

A good conductor knows how to direct the flow of silence in a great concert hall. But a great conductor, like Romanovna, knows how to deepen it, with a slow rise and soft sideward glance of her baton, with a lowering, a settling, a long-angled pause. She could feel the shift of energy moving through the hall, direct it, as if it were wind, or a cloud. She knew the subtle edges and flows of every mood, of every different shift and silent turn, and she knew how to hold and carry the entire audience deep and deeper into the pulsing pregnant silence that births everything, into the many different kinds of silence that river between all sounds, always.

As long as I live I will remember that evening, and the privilege of having been there for that concert, when I was taken, artfully, to the very depths of my soul, in a way that I had never experienced before and have never yet experienced again. And when I tell friends that I was at Romanovna's very last American concert before her arrest, trial, and execution, their jaws drop open in wonderment, and all of them always say to me, with deep envy, having watched the video of that evening over and over–all of them say to me what any devoted symphony fan would say of such an historic occasion–absolutely nothing.

The Ten Commandments
of Global Healing

BY IMAMAH JEROMA HIDAYATULLAH
OF COPENHANGEN
AND RABBAH DVORAH ROMELIA FROMM
OF MEXICO CITY

1–OUR WORLD IS A manifestation of a greater Oneness, participates in that Oneness, and is always a part of that great Oneness.

2–We have only one Earth, and we not will put our energy into anything that damages it or divides us from each other and all the life-forms with whom we share this world.

3–We will speak out against anything and anyone that does damage to the Earth and speak out for all those things which support its healing.

4–We will honor the cycles of work and rest, the rhythm of the seasons, the unfolding of this planet's wholeness, in our own lives and in the lives of all of humanity.

5–We will honor our parents, our families, and all the traditions of the world, for the wisdom of all our ancestors is a part of our shared heritage.

6–No war, no killing, of each other or the planet.

7–Integrity in all of our relationships, with each other and with the planet is what we strive for.

8–The abundance of the Earth has limits, which have been nearly reached, and all that still grows up from it is to be equally shared.

9–We always speak the truth, as kindly as possible, in every situation.

10–We will not make or use or purchase things that we do not need, that damage the Earth in any way, and that create imbalances in society, our communities, our families.

Noah and Naamah's Children

BY DORA HASSANI OF THE EDENIC RABBINIC COLLEGE
OF MOSCOW

This is the story
that always gets left out.
How the very first people
Eve and Adam and their children
all knew God
intimately.
They walked and talked with Him
and yearned for Him
when He wasn't around
like little children
waiting for Daddy
to get home from work
leaping up into His arms
with abandon and delight.

They forgave Him
when He shattered
the tower they built
to get close to Him
and scattered them
over the face of the earth

destroying the closeness
for each other
that they all once felt.
Yes
they forgave Him that
and forgave Him
the flood itself
those few survivors.

But what was unforgivable to them
began after the flood receded
when they walked in muddied landscapes
amidst the debris of ruined houses
seeing everywhere
the straining arms and hands
of the dead
reaching out for their salvation.

Even years later
Naamah and Noah's children
would come upon
the games and toys and bones
of the kids they played with
when they were small.
And it's that
that they could never forgive or forget.
It's that that makes us
keep our distance from You.
Not "backsliding"
as the Torah calls it
but inescapable and inevitable
mistrust and unforgiveness.

The Importance of Texts

BY RABBI SARA-ROSA IBN NURIEL

All of the books published by Rabbi Sara-Rosa during
her lifetime have survived: her monumental study of
good and evil in the rabbinic tradition, *The God of Undoing*, her collection of midrashim, *The Hasid and the
Hula Dancer*, a book of essays and sermons whose title
is a question, *Who Renews the Work of Creation Every
Day?*, as well as her text on Jewish Environmentalism,
Tasty is the Fruit on the Tree of Evil, which was published
in the year of her death. The following passage from the
uncompleted Talmud is sadly and strangely the only
complete surviving piece of her own writing from that
project.

The Editors

IN MANY SESSIONS OF our six gatherings so far, I've invited you to
stick as closely as possible to the discussion topic at hand, so please
bear with me when it seems that what I'm about to say veers off
from that topic, because I assure you that I will come back to it . . .
eventually.

When we look back at our long history as a people, historians
like my late mother suggest that we can see two energetic thrusts–
that of accomplishments and that of disasters. She saw both as
moving us forward in different ways, and saw our history of disasters as being like a series of stepping stones across a burning

84

lake–from enslavement in Egypt to the destruction of the First temple, from there to the destruction of the Second Temple and the Bar Kochba revolt, from there till the Expulsion from Spain, from there to the Holocaust, and from there till the birth and death of the State of Israel, not from war as might have been expected but from the entire region having to be abandoned due to it having become completely uninhabitable.

We as a people are used to disaster, to upheaval, to exile, to death. This is familiar to us, as part of our shared history and also part of our individual narratives. Many of us can tell stories about an ancestor who survived the Holocaust, or one who didn't. And this is layered over, woven through the ordinary human stories of tragedy–miscarriage, stillbirth, starvation, cancer, automobile accident, flood, fire, stroke, earthquake, plane crash, war, violence, heart attack, AIDS, MOT, RILF and all the rest of the modern viral plagues that we discussed in session yesterday, looking at the relevant texts that offer a communal background. But of course, in the story of our people and the Torah of our lives each one of us has their own personal tale to tell. And however horrible they might be, until now we have always been able to say–"Somehow we will go on. We always have, since antiquity." But now, now in this time of unprecedented disasters, our survival is not assured. The slogan of the post-Holocaust Era, "Never Forget," has been replaced by, "Who will be left to remember?"

A few weeks ago I was in Oakland visiting my daughter Chava and her family. After dinner I was sitting in the living room with my six-year-old granddaughter Naomi, just back from Hebrew School, who was sprawled out on the floor, crayons spread out around her, drawing. The drawing was clear. Two stick figures with breathing masks on were standing beneath a tree, a dry leafless desiccated tree, almost the only kind that she has ever seen. When I asked her what she was drawing she looked up at me and said, "Nanna, it's the last two people standing in the Garden of Eden."

The last two people. Where did she get that from? The last two people standing . . .

I couldn't have imagined–and I promise here that I'm spiraling back to the topic–I couldn't have guessed or imagined that global disasters would lead both to more war, on a small scale, and to far more peace than anyone of us could have ever hoped for. With some exceptions, and I won't repeat them, these nightmares by day and by night have brought out the best in all of us, hopefully not too late. And–one thing that's encouraged and sustained us in our work of global healing–has been our texts.

As Jews we probably all grew up thinking about what would happen to us, under this or that presidency, this or that regime. What we could not have predicted was that the Great Crash would severely damage our economy, new diseases would put–and I'm placing quotations marks around these words–"the fear of God" in all of us. And we could not have predicted that the Great Quake would seriously damage California and by domino effect the rest of North America in just the sorts of ways that often in human history have led to fear and blame and attack. And how odd, for us, with all of our texts ancient and modern–that this time someone else became the target and not us.

I remember reading a print version of *The Diary of Anne Frank* as a girl, I remember giving it to my daughter Noor when she was the same age that I was, and I remember her giving the very same battered copy to her daughter Zahava, may her memory be for a blessing, gone from MOT without having finished it. Perhaps in a few years my younger daughter Chava will give it to Naomi. We all know it, and as we discussed in an earlier session, while most of us would turn to other texts to read about that particular disaster, the book has a status that is almost canonical. And who could have guessed that somewhat more than a century after it was written that the book would once again become a companion and inspiration, in ways that would surely have horrified its young author.

This is what I want to say, that that one surviving textual artifact of a different time helped to engage all of us in the kinds of action that were not often enough done for us. Now that the Horrors are over, we can look back at ourselves with pride of accomplishment. Because I don't know a single synagogue, Hebrew

School, or Jewish Community Center whose basement and attic didn't become a hiding place for refugees. I don't know a single Jewish family that did not in some way aid in the survival of countless others. And while some of us had to travel some distance to be able to do that, we did, and I am proud of us.

My grandfather Alex told me that in his youth, in a time of discrimination and violence, that if you met another person who you thought could be gay you might ask them, "Are you a friend of Dorothy?" citing another important book in our cultural canon. And so it's been, in our lifetimes, that if you met someone and wanted to know if they were friend or foe, would work with you or turn you in, after chatting away for awhile you might say, casually, "You look familiar? Have we met before? Are you a friend of Anne?"

Texts in our time are important tools for survival. That is all that I wanted to say this morning.

Thank you.

Fragment 4

[. . .]
    When the Holy One
    Blessed be She
    Blessed be He
    Blessed be It
    Blessed be They
    (for so our text tells us by giving us 'Elohim'–a plural)
    awoke on the sixth day and got ready to go to work
    all the angels gathered around
    Her
    Him
    It
    Them
    and those angels
    seeing what was going to unfold that good day
    all said
    concerning the creation of the first human being
    "O Creator of all that is
    do not do this. Do not
    [. . .]

God's Devices

DR. STEPHANIE GILMAN, CAIRO RABBINIC UNION

ONCE, A GROUP OF rabbis were studying together in the Holy Land of Brooklyn.

Rabbi Jeremy said, "We read in *Pesachim 6b:* "There is no earlier or later in the Torah.""

Rabbi Yumiko said, "Rebbe Nachman wrote, "Sometimes one person speaks in one corner of the world and another person speaks in a different corner of the world, or one person speaks in one century and another person speaks in a different century, and God, who is above time and space, hears their words and connects them both.""

Rabbi Jeremy said, "That's why I think that when Rabbi Akiva asserted that *Song of Songs* is an allegory of the love of God for Israel–that he'd been reading Rumi."

Rabbi Rosalinda added, "That brings to mind the words of E. M. Forster: 'We are to visualize the English novelists not as floating down that stream which bears all its sons away unless they are careful, but as seated together in a room, a circular room, a sort of British Museum reading room—all writing their novels simultaneously.'"

Rabbi Christina replied with, "But aren't we forgetting Who It was Who first held in hand the mighty pen that wrote the Torah?"

Rabbi Kwame responded, "Isn't that the kind of androcentric, possibly even phalocentric thinking that we've been trying to . . . "

Rabbi Sebastian interrupted him with, "For me the big question is, thinking, not so much of God but of God's great scribe–was Moses a top or a bottom?"

Rabbi Fatima answered: "It says in *Exodus* that God showed His backside to Moses."

Rabbi Tina-Rob said: "That doesn't prove that God is a bottom and Moses was a top. It only suggests that . . . "

Rabbi Floella cut them off, saying, "I really can't believe we're having this conversation!"

Rabbi Christina asked, leaning across the table, earnestly: "I thought we were discussing the nature of text as it pours forth in revelation from God."

Rabbi Floella replied: "The whole Earth is full of His glory."

Rabbi Kwame interjected: "You mean *It's* glory!"

Rabbi Zeke answered: "The text tells us *His,* in every case. And you all know that!"

Rabbi Tina-Rob added, "Doesn't it actually say 'Elohim?' *Their* glory."

Rabbi Julio interjected: "Maybe His glory was Her strap-on."

Stories, Without Them

Collected in the cafeteria during Sessions Five Six, and Seven

BY TIMOTHY LEVY, THE FORMER MAGGID OF
BENSONHURST, BROOKLYN

THEY THOUGHT EVERYTHING WOULD be fine after the surgery.

Christine brought the challah.

Noboru was having an affair with Leora Mizrachi when he met Ross Alexander.

Listen, this is what Anna told Jabari.

And Juan even embezzled from his own brother.

No one could believe it when they heard that Jean-Gad had taken his life.

It took fifteen years and three plastic surgeons.

He dropped out of medical school–to do *what*?

It began on the afternoon of Memorial Day.

We stood there thinking–Those are the very last of our grapes. Ever.

Avnerah finally got her doctor to put her on a different med.

I still wonder how he ended up living on the street.

She kept the pistol behind some books in the den that belonged to her mother.

Her older brother told me that even before she left middle school she was doing drugs.

You can imagine Herschel's parents' reaction when he left Aviva for her sister.

After fifty-five years of marriage, three children, and five grandchildren.

He's diabetic, she's vegan, the baby's allergic to peanut butter. What should I feed them?

Please don't tell him that I told you, but his name used to be Sandra.

The teacher said he's somewhere in the spectrum, but not too severely.

Shanti didn't tell Zalman until after they were married.

First the prostate cancer, and now this.

We both use her recipe, but my sister Margot changed it. Only she won't admit it.

He began cutting himself right after the election.

They both knew the challenges of an open adoption.

Can you believe what he said to the imam?

That was the year we couldn't afford tickets for the opening game.

I saw him in Aruba, after he lost all that weight.

My mother was known for her cheerful disposition. But *we* had to live with her.

Thank God for Yumiko.

Right after the very last of the goats were gone.

His parents refused to go to the wedding, but Mother's mother came, in a red dress.

Okay, so they drank a bit too much. Is that a sin?

I just didn't want to see it.

We tried.

Not her pancreas, it was her liver.

And this is really your idea of life in our time?

A Panel Discussion: Why A Booth?

BY SHALLUM MARTINE LEFEY, PROFESSOR OF
ARCHETYPAL THOUGHT AT BIROBIDZHAN UNIVERSITY

PROFESSOR MOSKOWITZ: THE TRIBAL repetition of meaningful actions. Grounding the temporal in the physical. A recapitulation of our ancestors' first encounter with dislocation.

Professor Shirazi: Generation after generation, we build sukkahs because they shimmer in the liminal space between sacred and mundane.

Professor Schwartz: As a portal between the transitory and the eternal.

Professor Cohen: Between archetype and manifestation, Keter and Malkut.

Serach, a member of the audience, raises her hand: "Gentlemen, you've all got it wrong. The sukkah, humble, portable, impermanent, continues to exist–because it occupies the space between archetype and stereotype. One week out of Egypt, the rest of us were hot and dusty, tired, fed up, and complaining, while those two sweet gay boys Betzalel and Oholiab were painting their tent and decorating it, making dyes from plants and rocks they found out in the desert. At first, everyone laughed at them. 'Why knock yourselves out like this when we'll be back in Canaan in a few weeks?' But when we all finally got it, that we were going to be spending a long, long time in the wilderness, one by one the rest of us went to them for advice about how to make our own tents look nicer, feel nicer. And all those years later, after we got to Canaan and started living in real houses again, we still talked about how beautiful our tents were, out in the desert. And to remember them, year after year, when we were out in the fields with our flocks, or away from home, or on a pilgrimage, someone would set up their tent, or make a shelter, a lean-to, and decorate it the way they did, with flowers and fruit and fragrant branches. And long after we'd stopped living in tents, we still remembered Oholiob, Bezalel, and what they taught us. And when this story dropped out of the last edits to the Torah that we have now, we continued to make our little booths, huts, sukkot. So now you know the real reason why we set them up in our yards and on our terraces, year after year after year. Not because of liminality or numinosity, or anything fancy like that, but because of earthly beauty, and the enduring contribution of those two darling boys."

Professor Greenberg: "Madame, you are entirely out of place here."

Serach, looking up from her cellphone: "Madame, I have just texted you my resume—all three thousand years of it. And, a few more things to inform this discussion. The Torah says six hundred thousand men left Egypt. There were not many more than six hundred of us all together. Six hundred and twelve to be exact. At night we would sit around our flickering campfires, and Miriam would wander from fire to fire, telling us stories. That woman had a way with words. As for my adopted son and cousin Moses, he didn't have a speech impediment. He had a lisp which he was embarrassed about. And a good thing for the rest of us, as he was just a very dull speaker, unless the Spirit was upon him. Which didn't happen very often. And his brother Aaron wasn't much better. Too preachy for my tastes. No, it was Miriam who could talk. If only we'd preserved her stories. A tangle of Egyptian myths and Hebrew folktales. But sadly for all of you, her stories were cut from the Beta Version of the Torah, so you'll never get to hear them. Oh, and one more thing. When Moses found those two flat sparkly rocks in the desert and gouged those guidelines on them for us to follow, those same two boys, Ohoie and Betz, made a beautiful box for us to keep them in, with winged lions on top, sort of like Egyptian sphinxes. Their fancy box was what gave Moses the idea for all of us to make a tent to worship at, a miniature version of the temples we were used to in Egypt. Naturally he asked the boys to make it and decorate it. Fluttering in the wind, that tent was so beautiful, all pink and green and purple."

The Underground

By Dr. Jessica Markowitz-Kahana-
Abruzzi-Tagawa

We didn't expect it. We didn't expect what was coming. We didn't understand that certain prejudices endure, even underground.

We didn't anticipate it. We hadn't ever thought that our children would come to feel that their Jewishness, however remote, attenuated, ancestral, would begin to be seen as a disorder, one both genetic and psychological, social and even spiritual.

We discussed it in supervision and held a full-day conference three years ago to discuss the situation and seek solutions. Several of us wanted to approach it directly, but we lacked the resources to put together any kind of a handbook for other therapists. The notion that among our surviving children small groups would form in secret, small private gatherings that would make use of the standard literature of the Twelve Step Anonymous groups that date back to the 20th century–was simply unimaginable to us, and yet as you know that was exactly what happened.

We were horrified, even those of us whose Twelve Step work had been redemptive, healing, transformative. And we hesitate to say that in this horrible time–for approximately twelve percent of our attendants, doing the Steps worked completely at eradicating internalized anti-Semitism. For another thirty-seven percent the program worked for more than a year without any recidivism, and the same results for less than a year were documented in nineteen percent of those who regularly attended meetings.

The House of the Forgotten

BY RABBI SHULI BEN AVIVA V'LEAH

And Hagar gave birth to a son for Abram, and Abram called the name of his son whom Hagar had borne Ishmael. Genesis 16:15

And Abraham called the name of his son who was born to him, to whom Sarah had given birth for him: Isaac. Genesis 21:3

And Abraham went on and took a wife, and her name was Keturah, and she gave birth to Zimran and Jokshan and Medan and Midian and Ishbak and Shuah for him. Genesis 25:1–2

The second Edenic rabbi of Brooklyn, Carla Sarfati, taught in the name of her predecessor, the blessed Rabbi Moshe-Leah m'beit Goldberg:

We know the descendants of Isaac. Through his son Jacob, called Israel, and through Jacob's son Judah, we call them the people of Israel, or Jews. And we know the numerous descendants of Ishmael, the Arabs, and by extension, the Muslim peoples of the world. But what of the children of Keturah, whose six sons far outnumber Abraham's sons by Hagar and Sarah? Their names are a partial clue to their identities: nomadic tribes living in the Arabian Peninsula bore their names. One, Midian, was the ancestor of Zipporah, the wife of Moses. The rest are all obscure. Their mother's name, Keturah, is related to the word for incense, which may indicate that her sons lived along the incense trade routes of ancient times. Some midrashim identify her as Hagar, who Abraham reconnected with after Sarah's death, but there is nothing in the Torah to suggest this.

We know the descendants of Isaac. And we know the descendants of Ishmael. But who are the descendant of Keturah? Sent by Abraham to the East, toward the rising sun, I say that the six children of the House of Keturah scattered across the world, to every land, every continent, carrying with them their father's message of Unity. And I say that wherever people speak of peace and practice peace, they are the children of Keturah, spreading a sweet smell throughout the world. And I say that now, after ages of fighting and war among and between the children of Hagar and Sarah, that the time has come for the descendants of Abraham's six sons by Keturah to inherit the mantle of peace given to them by their father. Wherever they are, in whatever land, nation, race, or faith, let them step forward as teachers and prophets on the path of Unity, Unity for all of humanity. And we know that one of her descendants was Jethro the mentor and father-in-law of Moses. Most sources talk of him as a pagan, as a man who was not one of us. But I suspect that he was Abraham's true lineage heir, never enslaved, who carried on Abraham's teachings, passed them on to his children, who were able through Jethro to finally share them with the man who was raised in Pharaoh's house and the people who had been oppressed for so long and had forgotten their own history.

The Sabbath Queen Comes to Manhattan

BY Rabbi Karly Marina Kahn-Chen

heaven drips sweat and she descends from the clouds
in white spike heels and diamonds
turning on the town
in a low-cut dress
and dancing
over hydrant spray

with stars on her eyelids
and a rainbow tattoo on her thigh
over buses
on the street
on the IRT
and we go out to meet her
and we dance
till drunk dawn kisses her lipstick off

then she returns to the sky
still dancing
still turning
tropical August Saturday night

I Believe

By Rabbiner Irmgard Sara Baum

I believe with perfect faith in the coming of the messiah–
Moses Maimonides

On Yom Rishon everyone in the world woke up and said, "The world is a mess, but from now on I'm going to bring light to all the chaotic places." And they did.

On Yom Sheini, the day in which Goddix said twice of what was created that it was good, everyone in the world woke up realizing that we've polluted every body of water as well as the air. And everyone immediately began to find ways to stop doing those two things, from individuals to families to global corporations and even nations.

On Yom Shlishi everyone in the world woke up and said, "How did we ever destroy all the rain forests and almost every other form of vegetation?" On every part of the planet people began to sprout seeds, stopped using poisons on any growing things, and began to reforest the world.

On Yom Rivii everyone in the world woke up and didn't turn on the light beside their bed right away. No, they lay in bed thinking about all of the ways that we have misused energy to run things we don't even need. And they all got out of bed determined to stop doing anything that in any way harms the planet, which they did, from the humblest individuals to the heads of the most mighty nations, all of them recognizing that it would take quite some time to find whole new ways to live here, and utterly clear that having at last made this major shift that everything would slowly over time be all right.

On Yom Chamishi everyone in the world woke up to the silence around them, horrified that we'd driven birds and insects and almost all of the fish in the lakes and the rivers and the oceans to extinction, and they gathered together to create refuges and sanctuaries for endangered species, knowing that much was lost and knowing that their children's children would go to sleep at night to the sound of cicadas buzzing and would wake to songbirds singing in the branches of the trees outside their bedroom windows.

On Yom Shishi people all over the world woke up realizing that they could still save the mammals that are our closest relatives. And they sat up in bed horrified by the divisions we've created between ourselves, and they started giving things away and reorganizing the world in such a way that everything would be utterly and equally shared from that point on, so that everyone in the world lived comfortably, with no variation in anyone's income, teachers and factory workers and heads of corporations all earning the same amount.

On the evening of Yom Shishi, just before Shabbat began, everyone in the world spontaneously began dancing, singing, and discovering in themselves for the very first time exactly what it means for us to have been created in the image of Goddix. That joy and delight in being alive spread like a golden wave around the entire planet. And toward the end of the day, just before the beginning of Shabbat, every single person in the world who had a wireless device of any kind received a message from the messiah in their mother tongue in which she wrote, "Beloved ones, you have done such a good job internalizing my telepathic messages to you as I prepared for my arrival next week–that I am no longer needed here and shall instead incarnate on the planet Kluthric, which is found on the far edge of the galaxy and is in even more desperate need of help than you were. Thank you all for awakening, just in the nick of time. Oh, and please share this message with any neighbors, friends, and family who don't have a wireless device." So they did, which made for a glorious Shabbat, the very best in our history–so far.

Home

BY MAGGID BEATA ROMAN

THE BAY AREA HAS been my home for more than sixty-five years. I was born here, went to school in Jerusalem, moved back here and remained. For those of us who survived the Great Plague of 2087, spread by insects that thrive in our blistering heat, the Bay Area is unrecognizable. The bay is twice its former size. Half of San Francisco is under water, as well as all the coastal regions of California. But in spite of rising ocean levels, do you remember the last year in which we had any rainfall? Were you standing outside in the heat as I was, your face and open hands raised to the sky, laughing–your breathing mask left inside because you ran out to see and hear and feel it? Your head thrown back, your mouth wide open, wanting to catch and taste a few drops, or many–in a Paleolithic gesture swiftly aborted when those toxic drops began to sear your exposed lips and tongue. And that was the only time my grandchildren ever saw rain fall. That one single stretch of six and a half minutes in a single afternoon in June.

My little house clings to the top of the Oakland hills. Looking down on those rare clear days when I can see out, the abandoned towers of Oakland and San Francisco reach up from the water. My grandchildren love to hear stories about what it was like when I was their age, stories of busses and cars and stories of walking for hours up and down the verdant hills of spring and early summer. They laugh with disbelief when I tell them about scampering squirrels and runaway dogs, about birds winging their way across a cloudless sky. "Was the sky really blue then, Grandma?" they ask in wonder. I tell them yes, "As blue as your eyes, Chanah, and at night there were thousands of twinkling stars, as sparkly as *your* eyes, Trevor-Luis."

Fragment 5

[...]

. . . and then ze said, "If ever you want to understand the rituals of a Passover Seder or might want to gain some insight into the Christian Last Supper, and if you want to understand why so many rabbis from *Talmud* to *Zohar* are having conversations while they're out walking, go back and read Plato, especially *Symposium,* so that you understand our deep roots in classical homosexuality and . . .

. . . lost medieval Spanish love poems written by women to women, and secret medieval Spanish rabbis, all of them underground, who were women of a specific lineage ordained by other women, a lineage that goes back to . . .

. . . thinking of the monumentality of *Isaiah, Jeremiah,* and *Ezekiel,* we nearly all of us agreed that there are three more recent texts of nearly canonical status–Anne Frank's diary, Etty Hillesum's journal, and Elie Wiesel's *Night.*

Some said Allen Ginsberg, others Adrienne Rich, and a small faction said that to talk about books as if they are defining practices and not to mention the sacred texts of our own era–films–is to only tell . . .

[...]

Standing at the Open Door

RECORDED BY JULIAN BEN-AM, PROFESSOR OF SACRED
LITERATURE AT YESHIVA UNIVERSITY

THE MAGGID OF MANHATTAN said, "We know who stands at the open door. All of our ancestors, all of whom stood with Moses on that fateful day at Sinai."

The maggid of Denver said, "Going even further back, all the way back to Abraham our father and Sarah our mother."

The maggid of Chicago said, "Ours is a large tent, open on all four sides. We cannot forget the children of Hagar and the children of Keturah."

The maggid of St. Louis said, "Our tent is all of humanity. For are we not all the children of Noah, who with his good family survived disaster?"

The maggid of Atlanta said back to her, "We are all Eve's children. She is our first mother and that we must remember."

The maggid of Brooklyn said, in the name of his teacher Rabbi Beatrice Sclama, "This tent is the Shechinah. It is Her sheltering wings. It is Her carrying us aloft in sacred flight to the next world."

The maggid of Miami said, "We are Albert Einstein, we are Gertrude Stein, we are Barbra Streisand, we are Leonard Bernstein."

The maggid of Boston asked, "Are we Meyer Lansky? Are we Bernie Madoff?"

The maggid of Buffalo asked, "Are we Karl Marx?"

The maggid of Salt Lake City asked, "Are we yet Jesus?"

The maggid of San Francisco said, "We came out of Egypt a mixed multitude. Are we not of every race, and of each nation and color?"

The maggid of Los Angeles said, "Who stands holding open the welcoming door are those *gerim* who chose to join us, the blessed ones who were at Sinai with us but who do not share our particular genetic material. Among them, looking back in time, the blessed Marilyn Monroe, the blessed Elizabeth Taylor, the blessed Sammy Davis Jr., the blessed Julius Lester, the blessed Connie Chung."

The maggid of San Antonio said, "Must we count among the ranks of our people the Jewish descendants of Donald Trump?"

The maggid of Brooklyn said, "It is time for us to daven ma'ariv."

The Landscape of Heaven

BY Maggidah Chava Treeworthy

For some people, dear, it's a shock to realize that they are dead, especially those people who do not believe in an after-life. (Which is really a misnomer. Inter-life would be a better term, or pre-and-post life.) But whatever we call it, for people who do not believe in an afterlife, or a soul, well, it's quite a surprise to find themselves dead yet still existing. And then there are people whose lives were difficult, and who yearned to not exist, to be dead, to be un-done, non-existent. Some of them, after death, are quite delighted to be out of pain, out of the world. But other such people, like our dear cousin Jessie, are enraged when they get to this side and find that they still exist. She's been dead for years and yet each time we get together she says, "What an affront this is, to my integrity, to my intelligence." I just smile and nod and no longer ask her if she's still seeing her therapist.

For myself, I always imagined that I would go on, so a very short round of therapy had me back on my feet again, so to speak. But if you're one of those people who think that God, the angels, and everyone else in heaven speaks Hebrew, then you're in for a big surprise. No one does. We all speak a sort of telepathic language that everyone forgets when we are born, and remember again soon after we die and realize where we are.

Now if you ask me, being dead is actually quite easy; easier than being alive. Being born is like putting an ocean in a soda bottle. Dying is like breaking the bottle. You tell me which is easier.

And so many things are taken care of here that you have to do for yourself down there. Living in heaven is a bit like what I thought it might be like to live on a kibbutz, from what I've read about them, not that it doesn't have its challenges. For example, let's go back to language. What I found is that the hardest part of being dead, at least this time around, was remembering all the different pronouns. We were raised speaking English and we were accustomed to first person, second person, and third person, in either singular or plural. Dave, my disappointing third husband, once told me that Hebrew and a few other languages he knew had a dual form, but the languages I spoke did not. However everything is way more complicated in heaven, until you get the hang of it, the innate logic of it.

Here is a beginning lesson in Person. First, there is first person singular. That's simple: ME. But first person plural get complicated as there are three forms of it, but not just US. There's first person plural when everyone you're talking about is dead, like all your dead relatives. Then there is first person plural when everyone you're talking about is alive, like those you left behind. And then there is first person plural when the people you're talking about are a mixture of alive and dead. That's the form you use when you are talking about your entire family, in heaven and on Earth.

But if you've got first person down, don't think you've mastered personness yet, because First Person has one more layer to it. There's the first person pronoun you use when you are speaking of yourself, your individual self, the singular expression of the Over-Soul from which you emerged. And then there's the first person pronoun that the Over-Soul uses when it talks through you. If you haven't gotten that down yet, don't worry about it. It will all make sense when you are here. And if it's still confusing, they offer lots of classes, and all of them are free.

Second person has the same challenges, although singular is a bit easier. Plural is confusing. Is the group of people, the "you" that you're talking to, alive or dead or a combination of both? Same with third person. In Heavenish you have to be aware of your categories. For example, you're talking about a family member who is dead–so you use one form of the third person pronoun, or you're talking about a family member who is alive, and then you use another form. But when someone is dying, and you talk about how you went to their death bed, then you use another form entirely.

Now I'm trying to explain this to you in English, because I know, Masha, that it's the only language that you know. Okay, a little bit of Yiddish, a word or six. And some high school Spanish. And the few words you remember from Hebrew School and that summer when you spent a month on a kibbutz, back when–but do we really want to talk about that? No. But basically it's English I'm trying to translate all of my thought into, so be patient with me if I have to go back over a few concepts. I'm only doing this because you asked, because you want to get ready, because you want to be more prepared for being dead than I was when I was gone.

Do you remember that poem that Alexander wrote, when we were all in high school. High school. What a laugh. You and I were high all the time. He had no idea. And he moved there from New York. You'd think he would have known better. Poor boobie.

> The souls of the dead
> sit on their thrones
> asking each other
> the impossible question–
> "Is there a life after death?"

But let me get back to persons in language. First, second, and third. Singular and plural, although as I said, some languages have dual and other forms. But here's where it gets difficult when you're dead, darling. In Heavenish there is fourth person, singular, dual, triadic, quadradic, and plural, to be used when you are, are talking to, or talking about one deity, or two, or three, or four, or more than four. Got that? And then there's another form all together, but fortunately it only comes in one case, and that's fifth person, which is always singular. It's the case reserved for God Itself, or when It talks to Itself, or talks about Itself.

I know this is all confusing, and I'm sorry if you're overwhelmed. But you did ask me about all of this last night in a dream, and I'm doing my best to be a better sister now that I'm dead than I was when I was alive.

I Dreamed of Graves

by Maggid Beata Roman

It was the longest and most vivid dream that I ever had. The kind of dream you write down in your journal, and it takes an hour. The kind of dream that you tell your therapist and all your friends and family, and then talk about it for years and years, till all of them can tell it back to you. And if you never had such a dream, perhaps I wish one on you.

In the dream we are all living on the eastern shore of a very large lake, in a time that is both now and not now, a world that is both here and not here. To the south and north of us the land is rocky, too rocky for farming or the grazing of animals, rocky and surrounded by mountains. It is the same to the west. High mountains. No, the only habitable part of the entire lake is where we live.

No one knows how our ancestors got here. Or why. The elders tell us that they came from the far south, hundreds of generations ago, escaping a plague. Or was it a war? I can't remember which. We have neither here, and while I do know what they are, from the stories we tell about other places–I do not fear them.

I fear one thing only. Not my death or suffering or that of other people. It's all a part of life. What I fear is this. That once a year, and for about one month only, the rains used to come sweeping in across the lake. The rest of the year, it never rained at all. So all of our water for an entire year came from the rainwater we stored during that single month of the rainy season, in the cisterns that our people have been digging underground since first we came here all of those years ago. And of course we had supplementary cisterns for those years when no rain fell, or hardly any. Yes, we took care of all that.

My father told me the reason that we had no war here is that our life is so harsh that we must all cooperate with each other. We had to cooperate in order to create and maintain the underground cisterns in which we store the water all of our lives depend upon. Each village and town has its own cisterns, and every roof is covered with storage containers. All of them need to be repaired constantly. A teacher when I was small said that the reason that we have no plague here is that in spite of how scarce our water is, or perhaps because of it–we are clean, we are very clean people, so diseases don't spread.

Perhaps. Who knows. All that I know is that war and disease don't scare me, nor does hunger due to failing crops. We hear that other people in other places eat animals to survive, fish and birds and other living creatures. We do not, and I think it would scare me to eat one, to try and eat one–but not very much.

What scares me is that it has not rained in five years. The cisterns are about to become empty. We have stopped bathing and cleaning and all of our irrigation channels are about to run dry. But that does not concern me. Everything must come to an end. No, I do not fear the end of our life here. It has been a good life, and now it is ending. No, death does not scare me. What scares me is this–as one by one we are already dying, we are burying each other. They say in the old stories that two people in war can kill each other at the same time. I do not understand that, but it does not scare me. Sadden me, yes, but not scare me. What scares me is this–two people can talk to each other, two people can feed each other, two people make love to each other, two people can curl up and sleep side by one. In a dream within my dream, my husband and I once had the same dream. The very same dream. Yes, we were together in the same dream that we dreamed at the very same time. It was a sweet dream. We were having a picnic by the lake and a big flying creature flew by, something that neither of us had ever seen before, but when we woke up and described it to each other, we realized that we had had the same dream and seen the very same flying creature. He is dead now, my husband, dead from hunger, and yet I still wonder what that beautiful white long necked flying creature was in our shared dream.

Yes, sometimes two people can do that. Rarely. And two people can kill each other at the same time, they could strangle each other or use a knife or some of those other weapons that the old stories tell us about. Yes, there are so many things that two people can do together. Two people can sing together, dance together, and two can kill each other. Yes, two people can do that. But two people cannot bury each other at the same time. And that is what scares me. What if I am the next to the last one to die here, in our little village by a lake surrounded by mountains. And I bury the person who has gone before me. Yes, I do that. I bury that person, lovingly, shoveling all the dirt in the grave I dug myself for them. Yes, I can do that. I will do that, if things turn out this way. But here is what scares me. If I am the very last person alive in our little village of tall stone houses and blue tiled roofs—who will bury me?

Three Rabbis Were Walking

BY PROFESSOR TRUDY WARHAFTIG

THREE RABBIS WERE WALKING over the Brooklyn Bridge.
Some say it was the Golden Gate Bridge.
Some say it was four rabbis.
Others say it was a rabbi, a cantor, and a maggid.
My mother, when I was a child, here in Brooklyn, told me
that it was a rabbi, an imam, and a Catholic priest. In fact, she
claimed that she knew the priest, that he was the great uncle of her
best friend Connie Wallace from high school.

Three rabbis were walking over a bridge. It could have been
any bridge, it could have been anything that connects two places
that need to be connected. Some say it was Israel and Palestine.
Some say it was religious and non-religious Jews. Some say it was
the living and the dead. (That's my favorite version.)

Three rabbis were walking across the luminous bridge between this world and the next world. One of them was a man, one
of them was a woman, and one of them was both and neither.
The first rabbi said to the other two . . . actually, I forgot what
he said. And I forgot what the other two rabbis said back to him,
her, them. (Actually, I don't think it makes a bit of difference if it
was four rabbis, a rabbi and a cantor and a maggid, or if it was a
rabbi, an imam, and a parson, pastor, minister, or priest, Buddhist,
Hindu, Catholic or otherwise.)

Three male rabbis (Why not stick to the simplest version?) were walking across the luminous bridge between this world and the world to come. They were confident, comfortable, ready to be going there. None of them had a map, and they all kept wondering if they would remember the way—but because this is a fairy tale, of course they did, simply because it has to have a happy ending. (In some of the other versions they weren't all gay men, but in this version they are.)

Three aged men who were all rabbis and had all been married to other men, were slowly crossing the luminous bridge between this world and the next.

One of them stopped and said, "Oh. I forgot my sorrow."

Another one said, "Oh. I forgot my hat."

The third rabbi said, "I seem to have forgotten my name."

All three turned around, wanting to go back. But such is the nature of that bridge that with each step you take the bridge vanishes behind you. And thus, they found their way to heaven, missing a few things, but very happy to be there. And great big aqua-colored angels greeted them and made them feel quite at home.

Alas, I forget what happened after that, but isn't it enough to have gotten them that far, in a time of massive global extinctions and horrifying daily deprivations?

(Oh. Now that I think back on it, I'm certain that it was the beautiful Brooklyn Bridge that they were crossing.)

A Counter-Dayenu

BY RABBI RONIT GOLDWOMAN FROM HEBREW UNION
COLLEGE IN DENVER

IF OUR STORIES HAD been told in the Torah, it would not have been enough.

If our stories had been told but we had still been called an abomination, it would not have been enough.

If our stories had been told but we had still been called an abomination, an abomination punishable by death, it would not have been enough.

If our stories had been told but we had still been called an abomination, an abomination punishable by death, and if there had been no apology to us for all the years of our suffering, it would not have been enough.

If our stories had been told but we had still been called an abomination, an abomination punishable by death, and if there had been no apology to us for all the years of our suffering, and if we were still not included in the total fabric of our people, it would not have been enough.

But if our stories had been told, and we had never been called an abomination, an abomination punishable by death, and if there had been no need for an apology to us for all the years of our suffering because we had always been included in the total fabric of our people, free to live and love and fulfill our destinies in the image of God, then and only then would it have been **dayenu,** enough.

The Return

BY MAGGID BEATA ROMAN

I FOUND A BOX in the attic of the big house looking out on the harbor that we were preparing to abandon, a house that members of our family had lived in for four generations. My sister Irma and our brother Luis and I were doing the packing, although I was still in mourning for my wife Violet, who'd died in the SIF epidemic. The city had given everyone six months to evacuate before the water levels rose too high for anyone to live on Staten Island, situated as it is on the outer side of the great Hope Dike completed two years before, to protect Manhattan, the Bronx, and Brooklyn from the rising sea, the single largest and most expensive public work in all of human history.

Of course, we'd left everything till the last minute. My daughter Carla had offered to help, but she was trapped in Winnipeg, where she manages a factory that packs the ice and the snow that still falls in winter to ship to other locations. It had been a reasonably snowy winter–six inches fell and remained on the ground– and there was no way that she could leave in the middle of the snow harvest.

The three of us were nearly done packing when I came upon the small wooden box, slipped under the eaves behind a small cardboard box full of old worn books. The books were moldy; we went through them and agreed that we would throw them out. But the box, the small wooden box whose lid was carved with spiraling branches, contained a great secret–two pages of brittle yellowed paper, neatly folded, one on top of the other. The one on top was a certificate in Hebrew and in English, dated January 15, 1936, and signed by three male rabbis, certifying that our grandmother had completed all of her rabbinic studies and was now officially a rabbi. The rabbis were Morris Fishman, Jacob Kaplan, and Eli Markowitz.

"Did you have any idea?

"I can't believe it."

"This is a secret that we were surely meant to find."

"From a grandmother we never even knew we had."

"An artifact–from our own private genizah."

"Genizette."

"It gives me the willies. Like she was some kind of spy, living with us all the time, but hiding."

"It's amazing."

"Did either of you know that Grandma was more than just a plain old Hebrew School teacher?" Luis asked.

Irma and I, the eldest, shook our heads from side to side.

"I feel like we're getting her back."

"A different Grandma, all resurrected."

"Resurrection is Christian, Luis."

"Reincarnated."

"That's Buddhist."

"Damn it, you know what I mean!"

Below the certificate was a letter:

"To whomsoever finds the document that accompanies this letter, please note that it is authentic. Please note too that I have never intended it to be seen by anyone till after my death. You who are reading these words now, perhaps my descendants, please note that my private ordination was intended to be such by the three good Orthodox men who signed the certificate you have found here. And please note that their decision to grant smichah to me in secret was intended to be an act of faith, a gesture of hope, the planting of a seed for the future.

We had all heard about the ordination of Regina Jonas in Germany in December of 1935, and it was their intention for me to be the first American woman to be so ordained. There was however much opposition to their decision in the local community, hence the ceremony was done in private. We were living in a difficult time and waiting for a better time, but the situation in Europe grew worse and worse, they didn't want to create controversy in our beleaguered community, so we continued to keep my ordination a secret. Then the bombing of Pearl Harbor happened, the United States entered the Second World War, and in the aftermath of the war so much else in our world needed to be tended to, those three good men had all gone, so I kept on doing what I'd long been doing, and never said a thing.

When I first heard about Sally Priesand, I thought about bringing forth this document, but so much time had gone by, so many losses, and I didn't want to do anything to detract from her great achievement. But I am old now, and rather than attract attention to myself, even at this late date, I've tucked this letter and my certificate in a box where I know that someone will eventually find it, my children or grandchildren perhaps. When you do, please note that my ordination in Brooklyn was a great honor, a source of endless private joy, and yet something that I did not even share with my dear and beloved husband, whom I met and married several years later. And please ask yourself as you read this, what else has been forgotten, what else has been lost, what else must be regained if we as a people are going to survive."

The letter, written in a shaky hand, was signed by our grandmother, Bella Roman.

Two Teachers from Many

BORINA KAVA, MAGGID OF SAN JUAN, PUERTO RICO

Mid-morning presentation for Session Five

WHAT CAN WE LEARN from them, those two such different characters? I ask as a great fan of cartoons and animation, as a voracious
reader in childhood of the fables of Aesop, who had (dare I mention it?) a great fondness in childhood for those curious animal-
headed deities of ancient Egypt.

I am certain that the ideas for cartoons–Mickey Mouse,
Porky the Pig, the Teenage Mutant Ninja Turtles, and Greta the
Purple Giraffe (a stuffed version of which was my sleeping companion for many years)–weren't invented in the 20th century but
are encoded in us–witness Aesop and similar tales once told all
around the world. As a teenager I loved those Native American
tales of Coyote the Trickster. Yes, I am certain that the ideas for
creating such images in cartoons are a fundamental part of our
DNA, that cave people long before there were ancient Greeks or
Hebrews were telling stories about talking horses and bison and
elk and bears.

So what can we learn from the only two talking animals that
we are given in our most sacred text, the Torah? What can we learn
from the talking male snake in "Bereishit" and the talking female
donkey in "Balak"? On the surface it's quite simple to say that the

first is bad, a wicked tempter, while the second is good, a patient caring guide. There are so many midrashim written about both, the snake and the donkey, the serpent and the ass. But there are times when it behooves us to consider the fact that the stories in the Torah are often themselves midrashim on older stories, stories that are now lost to us. So we may consider that the serpent is a potent guide to our evolving humanity, the one who awakened our ancestors to higher reasoning, as might have been reflected in more ancient stories, perhaps of a great mother goddess whose totem was, not a phallic serpent, but an umbilically connecting snake. And perhaps the talking donkey that guides Balaam in our story may also have been, true to the at-times feisty nature of such beasts, not only a wise traveling companion but also a nasty intrusive commentator on her master's limited perceptions.

Two, and only two talking animals in our most sacred text, certainly stand out. One might say that because of their uniqueness we are required to confront them, to investigate them, to dance with them in our imaginations. The male snake and the female donkey. The bad and the good. Two talking animal guides in our collective verbal cartoon series. What would happen if we put the two together, as their uniqueness almost demands? What kind of a story would we tell, if that serpent met the donkey on the road? Both of them guides, one negative and one positive if we stay with a plain reading of the text. Why do we meet the evil tempter first, in that garden? And why do we meet the goodly guide second, on that snaking path through a vineyard? There are angels in both stories, cherubim to keep Eve and Adam out of the garden, and that singular angel who encounters Balaam and delivers a message to him, as all angels are required to do. And there are swords in each story. The cherubim carry them in the first, while Balaam draws his in the second.

Can you see the animated version of these two stories? Can you imagine the way in which a good storyteller sitting around an ancient campfire brought them to life with her artful evocative words, perhaps long before those two stories were ever written down? What do you make of the recurring elements? Surely, even in two stories so widely spread apart in the written text, they are intentional literary/visual devices. And certainly, in these two ancient teaching tales, we have even more to learn–but this is all the time that I was allotted for this session, so I invite you to go back to these tales and read them, one after the other, and see what comes forth to meet you on the pathway towards understanding.

Thank you.

The City of Light

BY MAGGID BEATA ROMAN

IT WAS A CHILDHOOD dream to go, but I've never been there. The United Nations was born in San Francisco, but it settled in New York, the International Court of Justice is in The Hague, and so many eyes of the world were turned toward Jerusalem in thoughts and in prayers. But it seems to me that if Planet Earth was ever to have a capital city, it would have been Paris. Think of all the love songs: "The last time I saw Paris her heart was warm and gay." "I love Paris?" "April in Paris." And perhaps my favorite, "Free Man in . . . " you know where. Think about all the books about it, not all by French authors, including Hemingway's *A Movable Feast*. In a film, even a momentary flash of the Eiffel Tower in the distance sets the scene. Paris and lovers, Paris and food, Paris and art. Paris–the height of civilization.

But now, near the end of the 21st century, I remember those images of Paris, no longer called the City of Light but the City of Darkness. It's now and for the rest of time the city of the tormented hunchback of Notre Dame, the city of Nazis marching beneath the Arc de Triomphe, and it's the city from the first film version of H. G. Wells' book *The War of the World*–destroyed by Martians.

In a horrible way, how much more comforting that would have been, to hear in the news that aliens had destroyed our most perfect city, and not we ourselves. "A nuclear incident, accident," we call it. Not a terrorist attack. A city obliterated. Accidentally. The images–biblical. Worse than anything that poor Noah and his

family saw when they staggered out of their ark. Almost everything leveled: Notre Dame, the Arc du Triomphe, the Louvre. The
Eiffel Tower's sad melted remains sticking up from blown rubble.

My mother told me about her honeymoon trip there with her
first wife. How lovely it was, how perfect, how beautiful. The songs.
The buildings. The dogs on leashes everywhere. The people, the
food, the history, the light. The endless museums. The marvelous
way in which the artifacts of many, many centuries sat side by side,
a medieval church and a modern glass tower. Whereas now, when
we hear the word "Paris," what we think of is rubble, radioactive
for thousands of years.

Fragment 6

[...]

And to the topic of this session–"Do we need to believe in any kind of a Supreme Being to be part of a Jewish conversation?" I would like to say that

[...]

But for me there is no difference between a personal God and an impersonal one. They are part of Its dance of transcendence and immanence.

The *Torah* tells us that God hides His face from us sometimes.

Most of my congregants are happy to label as God that which they see as the vast singular energy field that contains everything in existence.

No. We must come back to something more defined, not necessarily theistic but

[...]

the opposite. After all that we've gone through, and looking at the state of the nation and the world today, there is really no point in

[...]

Buddhist, Sufi, certainly. They lead us to common ground. But as my teacher, Rabbi Tina-Rob likes to say

[...]

When the First Woman was Ordained

READ BY RABBI CHAVA-MARIA BARZILAI AT
FOLLOW-UP SESSION 14, GATHERING 2

WHEN REGINA JONAS WAS ordained, in Berlin in 1935, Rabbi Stein-Yi said that all the women in ancient times who had been the heads of synagogues, some of whose names have been preserved, surrounded her, including Rufina of Smyrna, Sophia of Gortyn, and Theopempte of Myndos.

Rabbi Karlinsky said that four great angels of light gathered around her.

Rabbi Herschel said that they wept.

Rabbi Kahn said that they laughed.

Rabbi Abouav said that they applauded.

Rabbi Levy said that they were outraged.

Rabbi Menashe said that one wept, one laughed, one applauded, and one looked a bit puzzled and then turned away.

Rabbi Rodriguez said of those four angels that one wept and then applauded, one laughed and then cried, one turned away not in puzzlement but disdain, while the fourth angel embraced her as it had in days of old embraced the women who were leaders in our communities.

When Sally Priesand was ordained in 1972 in Cincinnati, four great angels of light surrounded her, the same four who had gathered around Rabbi Jonas.

Rabbi Cohen said, "There are no angels."

Rabbi Solomoni said, "There were angels then but there are no longer angels in our time. They have withdrawn to heaven due to our failings."

Rabbi Smith-Cohen said, "I saw them, and they were laughing."

Rabbi Montez said, "They cried, one from sorrow and three from joy."

Rabbi Levy-Chan said, "They stood quietly around her with their wings spread wide, creating a shelter spacious enough for all of the women rabbis yet to come, and the gay and lesbian rabbis, the trans rabbis, the gender-queer rabbis, and the rabbis whose identities we don't yet have words for, and probably now never will."

While Rabbi Barncastle said, "Finally."

To which Rabbi Jonas added, "Yes. I've been waiting."

My Grandchildren

BY MAGGID BEATA ROMAN

THEY WATCH A LOT of old movies. They always ask me what it was like to be able to run freely outside, to go to the beach and lie in the sand with nothing to cover our bodies. At first, they didn't understand *how* people could do that. All they know is a world gone hot, a world where they imagined that the sand would be burning hot, as well as the air. When they got older they understood that the world wasn't as hot as it is today. That's a hard concept to grasp, like finally understanding that your parents were once children like yourself, and even your ancient grandparents. As little children we live fully in the present moment, a capacity we may spend our entire lives trying to get back to through various meditation practices. Yes, as children we all live fully alive and present in the present moment–a moment that we think is eternal, never-changing. And then gradually they, we, realize that change does happen. That this endless summer of our lives, which seems to go on and on and on forever, is really only two months out of a year. A year in which we can watch movies about people several decades ago lounging about on blankets, picnicking, laughing, in shorts and tee shirts in a park. Or, back to the beach, splashing in skimpy bathing suits in the water, wearing wetsuits not because the air outside is dangerous to breathe or to have contact with your bare skin, but because the water was too cold to be comfortable surfing in, riding waves too toxic now to ever stick your bare feet in them, not that anyone who isn't suicidal would be foolish enough to do that.

No, at first my grandchildren didn't understand that. But now they do, they fully grasp it. And they hate me for it, as if it were my fault that the world they watch on wall-screens, people as large as life, were living in a world that I destroyed myself, "On purpose," the youngest one said recently. "You did it on purpose. Destroyed the world. So that no one else could enjoy it."

I think of Noah. I think of my grandmother, roasting a chicken for dinner. I think of her stories of the Nazi concentration camps that her mother survived. I think of the stories I heard and read about Hiroshima and Nagasaki. A disaster here, a disaster there. A nightmare here, a nightmare there. All so contained. And to my dismay–I find myself jealous.

Havdallah for a New Era

BY PROFESSOR DELINA MATUIN OF THE EDENIC RABBINICAL COLLEGE IN COSTA RICA

HOW DO WE PRACTICE in these times, of fear, disease, poverty, and environmental degradation and decay? How do we honor a day of rest when there is so much work to do, and how do we end that day when most of the basics of our ancient rituals are denied us? Candles–have become rare. Paraffin is far too costly. Beeswax no longer exists as almost all of the world's bees are gone. Spices for a spice box? Most of the ones we used can no longer be grown or if they still grow are so rare and expensive that almost no one can afford to use them, and those who can, would not do so in any public way. Wine was so long a part of all of our rituals, marking their beginnings, at Shabbat, at Pesach, and on other occasions. I remember having had it a few times when I was a very little girl–a tiny sip from a cup passed around the table–but my children have never once tasted it, since the last grapes in the world stopped producing several decades ago due to climate change and the remaining plants all were gone due to invasive parasites, and the wines that still exist are so expensive that no one I know could ever afford a bottle, although a neighbor told me he went to a wedding where two hundred people sipped from a single bottle. True, many other plants have survived, and some thrive on this much warmer earth, and new ones are appearing, like this little poke-pine springing up from the soil I planted it in and brought with me in this little pot.

Sometimes we evoke the ancient ritual of welcoming in Shabbat. We did it here last night. We do it every week at home. We invite those gathered around the table to close their eyes and imagine that there are candles burning in the two old brass or glass or silver candlesticks that may have belonged to a great great grandmother, some of them still caked with wax drippings, those hardened streaks of dusty-white not something to be cleaned off but now cherished. Yes, we conjure what was. The burning candles. We pass around an empty silver cup that once held wine, as old in its provenance as those time-battered heart-treasured candlesticks. We think of the pictures and film images we've all seen, of people reciting the blessings, and we imagine ourselves into them, into the past, and into a future that is as evanescent as a dream.

We do the same at the end of Shabbat, with Havdallah. We conjure a colorful braided candle in its silver holder. We again imagine the smell and the taste of the wine, evoking it on our tongues, thick and syrupy sweet. Then we pass around our treasured spice boxes. We pass them around from hand to hand, lovingly, those empty silver, brass, ceramic or wooden containers, some of which, even after decades of being empty, still carry the faint, faint odor of nutmeg, cinnamon, and the other spices that once rested there, waiting for us to inhale them. Or we inhale the faint scents of the plants we use to replace the traditional ones, the few scented things that still grow that we can afford, that we may plant in the single flower pot we pour our cooking water into to keep alive. We do this to separate, to keep alive, to infuse our days and nights with the beauties of our tradition.

This evening, as the last light of day fades behind dark ominous clouds, those three stars seen in the sky that mark the end of Shabbat are almost never seen anymore. We gather around to end our day of rest–but to mark this end I invite us all to participate in a new ritual, a ritual based upon the old one, but altered as everything is altered, for our own time.

Havdallah means Separation. In this frightening time, we cannot afford any longer to be separate from anything that still survives. Not from each other and not from the earth. So instead of separating ourselves, instead of separating the sacred from the profane, of separating Shabbat from the rest of the week, I am going to conjure up for us at the end of this Shabbat a different image, one grounded in the work of our kabbalistic forbears in Safed–not a time of separation but a time of Yichud–of Unification.

Close your eyes for a moment and feel your breath. In this darkness, feel that all of us are one, that all the world is one, battered and yet one. Feel the great Oneness beyond, behind, and within all of our differences, and breathe that Oneness in to all of your cells.

I know that some of us in our rituals make use of a battery-operated candle. But, thinking of the traditional braided candles our grandparents and their grandparents passed around their tables, I am going to pass around a piece of colorful braided rope made by my daughter Rivka-Michael. Havdallah as it was practiced in the past was a joy for all of the senses, for sight and taste and smell. Please caress this multicolored braid when it comes to you, stroke it and let your fingers rejoice in it, rubbing it over and over again till you can't tell the difference between it and your fingers, till there is no difference, till your body remembers that all is one, that we are one–and then pass it on.

We do not have spices as did our families in times passed. Not the same spices. But we have others, we have new spices, ones that are springing up in abandoned fields, struggling to stay alive, delightful mutants that put out a potent new smell for their kinfolk to discover–with the pure biological hope that their drifting pollen will allow them to survive. Into my great grandmother Zahava's spice box, which she made herself, in a pottery class in college–into this colorfully painted and glazed and baked jar I have put some poke-pine that grew up in our barren backyard, a dried false-rose blossom that a neighbor gave me, and a sprig of one of the hardy plants from the past that still seem to thrive, a sprig of rosemary. Bury your face in them. Inhale, inhale deeply and become filled with the fragrance, become one with the smell.

Now, in the darkness, I will pass around an empty cup, goblet, chalice, an empty vessel. Or, is it empty at all? Is it not filled with the same air we breathe, toxic and yet still potent enough for us to survive? As I pass this not-empty cup around, lower your face into it and breathe, in and out, breathe in and out the blessedly filtered air that we are fortunate enough to be able to breathe in this building. Good. Now that the cup has gone around the circle once, I want to pass it around again. This time I invite you all to lean your face again into the cup and deposit there a bit of spit.

We are standing here tonight in the Holy City of Brooklyn, up at its highest point, high on a hill, on land where three centuries ago a great battle was fought during the American Revolution. Today we are all fighting a very different kind of battle, as we look down below us to the rising waters that are eating away houses and warehouses, streets, yards, and land. Rain either comes rarely these days, or comes too often and too fiercely. But even so, there is no separation between the water in our bodies and the water that we all just spit into this chalice, married together in this silver cup. Nor is there any separation between the water in this goblet and the water in the clouds, no separation between the water in the clouds and the water in the Hudson River that flows nearby, no separation between the river and harbor, between the harbor and the ocean, and no separation between the ocean and the One who created it. Nor can there be, in this new world, any separation between male and female, night and day, sacred and profane, nor any separation between Shabbat and the rest of the week.

May the joy we felt and shared over the course of this Sabbath day ripple out into the future, carrying us with no separation from now until the next Shabbat. And now, with love and gratitude, I will pour forth the joined and mingled waters of our bodies into this little terra cotta flower pot, to water and feed this little odd new plant, this little shoot of poke-pine that my grandson brought into the house for me to transplant. That tickled his nose when he took off his face-mask in the house so that he could smell it. That made him laugh. And made me laugh along with him.

Shavua tov. May this new ritual be for a blessing.

Fragment 7

[...]

If no kosher, it is acceptable to eat halal.
If no halal, it is permitted to eat vegetables.
If no vegetables, it is permitted to eat anything.
[...] permitted to eat treif.
Rabbi Sulman says, "Never."
Rabbi Yossi says, "Of course. Always."
Is it different if it's a child or an adult?
If no food [...]
"On the very last [...]

A Night at the Movies

BY RABBI ADINA YOHANNA OF CONGREGATION BETH
SHALOM IN SALT LAKE CITY

When Moses went up on high, he found the Holy One sitting and tying crowns on the Holy letters. He said to the Holy One: "Ruler of the Universe, who's holding back Your hand?" The Holy One answered: "There's a man who will appear at the end of several generations. Akiva ben Joseph is his name, and he'll need these crowns, because from each and every one he'll derive scores and scores of laws." Moses said to Him, "Ruler of the Universe, show me this man." The Holy One said, "Turn around!" Moses went and sat down behind eight rows. Not being able to follow their arguments he was uncomfortable, but when they came to a certain subject, the disciples said to the master 'How do you know this?' and he replied 'It's a law given to Moses at Sinai' and he was comforted.

From *The Babylonian Talmud, M'nachot 29b.*

Moses and Akiva found themselves sitting in the back row of a movie theater in Bensonhurst in Brooklyn, the old one on 86th Street. I forget the name. They were watching *Fiddler on the Roof,* which they wouldn't have understood at all as neither of them speak English–but there are a lot of Israelis living in the neighborhood, so the film had been dubbed into Hebrew, most of which they could understand, in spite of the changes in grammar and vocabulary, and in spite of the very odd accents.

"Remember," Akiva whispered to Moses as the opening credits rolled, "that this is the most famous film ever made about our people."

Moses nodded and a little while later leaned over and quietly asked his companion, "Are you sure they're children of Israel?" It was during the opening song, "Tradition," but nothing that they were singing about was familiar to him, was part of *his* tradition. He remembered his and Akiva's early conversation about what he'd been given at Sinai, but all of this just seemed too far away. Akiva could sense that and wondered if it was a mistake to take Moses to see for his first movie so alien a film, one about Ashkenazi Jews, creatures that he had barely ever heard of before. Maybe a play would have been better, he thought. Perhaps a stage version of this one, or maybe a revival of *The Zulu and the Zayde*, a short-lived and long-forgotten masterpiece that was one of his personal favorites.

Responding to the look of puzzlement on Moses's face, Akiva smiled at him and said, "Of course I'm sure they're children of Israel. True, they're as different from me as I am from you, and as different from the people surrounding us as we both are," he added, nodding over at a young man loudly cracking sunflower seeds and tossing the shells on the floor. "And yet, Moses, they are still our people, your people, God's people."

"I recognize the beards, the fringes on their garments, and even a few of their rituals. But the singing? It makes no sense to me, Akiva."

Akiva turned to his companion, lay a gentle hand on his forearm and said, compassionately, "I know that you were never fond of public speaking, and even less so of singing, but settle back and relax and enjoy the story for what it is, and I think it will start to make sense to you, in the same way that spending time in my classroom did." He didn't add that this was the fifth time that he was watching the movie.

Absorbed in the story himself, the next time that Akiva turned to his friend he found Moses nodding his head to the music. It was the song, "Miracle of Miracles," when Motel and Tseitel celebrate the good new that they will soon be married. Sensing Akiva's gaze, Moses turned to him, smiling. "This Tevye, he reminds me of Jethro, my father-in-law. Both wise and foolish at the same time." Akiva grinned, aware of his friend's modesty, for one of the lines in that song referenced Moses softening Pharaoh's heart, but Moses hadn't mentioned it. Then to his friend's delight, Moses laughed out loud during Tevye's imaginary dream, when he convinces Goldie his wife that it would be wrong to marry off Tzeitl to a rich older butcher rather than to Motel, the man she's in love with. Akiva liked that scene too. He'd been keeping a dream journal for almost two thousand years and always appreciated it when a dream appeared in a story, in any kind of a story—a sacred text, a book, a play, or a film, in 2D, 3D, or hologram.

The wedding scene, the two whispered to each other, was initially puzzling to both of them, as the wedding traditions were so far from what either of them knew, but neither could resist the sentiments behind the song "Sunrise, Sunset" and were carried away by the music. The sudden shift after that was startling. Both of them were familiar with hostility and violence being directed at their, at our, people. But both of them laughed at the scene of Goldie and Tevye admitting to each other that twenty-five years after an arranged marriage they realize that they love each other. Later, when another of Tevye's daughters, Hodel, sings of her leaving home to join her husband in Siberia, out of the corner of his eye Akiva could see Moses wiping away his tears. Later he could sense his companion's inner turmoil as they watched Tevye refuse to allow another daughter to marry a non-Israelite. He could feel thousands of years of his own life and of that of so many of our people stirring in Moses's body.

The closing number, when all of them have to leave their homes in Anatevka again brought tears to Moses's eyes, and to Akiva's as well, the two old men awash in memories. As the final credits rolled Moses turned to his friend and said, "Now, exile is something that I understand. It's a story that was told to me at Sinai." Akiva laughed and then they went across the street to his favorite kosher Chinese restaurant.

Fragment 8

[...]

    . . . if there was a Jewish father but not a Jewish mother."

    Rabbi Scharfen said, "I thought we'd already agreed on this. In our time, if either parent is Jewish. Mother or father. We go back to the Torah on this, back before Oral Law and its traditions."

    Rabbi Wein said, "Yes. In this time we must obey the law of Torah that states its teachings are for life and not for death."

    Rabbi Suleim said, "What if in that place there are none left who are Jews to be a parent, not women nor men nor others?"

    Rabbi Lukas-Kahn said, "A child who . . .

    [...]

A Tale for Tara Hannah Goldwasser, my Buddhist Grandmother

BY RABBI PINCHAS BEN SHAUL V'REUVEN

ELIEZER SAT BY THE sea, an old man. The day was hot, a listless breeze rose up from the docks, the beach. His new first granddaughter toddled by, laughing. The sea was sparkling. The ships in the harbor were rocking back and forth. His son Abner's wife called to him from the house, but he did not hear her. He was somewhere else, remembering, remembering the young man he used to be.

He was weary, not sure that he could go on, after weeks and weeks of walking, to the east and to the north, first with a caravan from his village, one that he joined in secret while his family slept, for they had forbidden him to leave. That first caravan passed him on to another when they stopped, then another, and in each village they came to, he would ask for information about the new teacher, leaving the coast behind and then, following their instructions, walking north and further north, alone.

The terrain kept changing. Plants and trees changed as he left Cochin and headed into the interior. Villages looked different from his own, and the languages the people spoke in those villages grew less and less familiar. But through shared words, gestures, and the almost telepathic communication that travelers discover within themselves, he was guided onward toward the new teacher, the one who had been awakened.

He remembered a hot day and a listless breeze coming down from the mountains that vanished into the trees above him. At the far end of the clearing, sitting on a slight rise, the teacher was speaking. He was a handsome man of middle years, with broad ruddy cheeks and large dark eyes, speaking a language he'd never heard before, that one of the merchants in the caravan told him was called Magadhi. A large circle of disciples was sitting around the teacher, and as he approached, the teacher looked up at him, his dark eyes smiling, and motioned him forward. He bowed, and the teacher asked him his name: he understood that. And he said it, knowing how strange it sounded in that clearing: "Eliezer ben Shmuel." The teacher smiled and asked him, with his face, his hands, his inner voice, what language he was speaking, and he nodded when Eliezer said "Hebrew," a language he knew the teacher had never heard of, who had paused in the middle of a story to greet and to welcome him, paused just as his grandmother used to pause, to think, to gather words together like a cook gathers together her ingredients to stir into a pot.

We all tell stories, Eliezer thought. Stories are what hold us together, stories are what make us human, although birds pip and chip and chatter and sing, and dogs bark and bay, cats meow, monkeys leap from branch to branch and they chatter and screech and hoot and howl, although there were none in the trees above him now. And dolphins squeak and whistle, and I remember Uncle Manasseh, just back from a long trip to the homeland, telling me that whales tell stories too, stories which echo out across the seas. And even the trees seem to be speaking, when the wind rustles their leaves, as they are doing now.

He thought, as the teacher smiled at him, his smile a great question, he thought of all the stories of his life, of his family, of his people. The stories his grandfather first told him. "We come from far away. We are merchants. We sell incense and perfume and unguents and spices, for people covet them in our homeland across the sea. And although others may be dying, and war may be raging, those among us who have money, and some always do–they need those precious things that come to them from afar. Which is why, hundreds of years ago, our great King Solomon sent his ships here from our homeland, to bring back to his capital city the perfumes and unguents and incense and spices for his wives and his priests in the great temple he built to our one Great God. For a pound of our incense costs more than twenty slaves. And we settled here, welcomed by the king, and we stayed here, and we pray here, still and always turning toward our holy city of Jerusalem, and we bow, not to the goddesses and gods in the temples of our neighbors, but to our One God, who lives far away in that land, that land whose great and holy temple was destroyed in the time of my dear departed father."

Eliezer remembered that as he took a seat at the edge of the teaching circle. A family of monkeys leaped into the tree above him, chattering wildly, interrupting his reverie. He wanted to laugh, but restrained himself. For the teacher had closed his eyes and began to chant. And his students were chanting, chanting, chanting. He could not understand then what they were saying–he would later–but he felt them, the chant so different than the ones he knew from his own people, and yet they touched him, deeply.

He came back to the day, as his granddaughter came toddling back along the beach, shrieking with laughter in the way that little girls do. He laughed too, and went back to his reverie.

He'd stayed there for two years with the new teacher, the enlightened one. Then, feeling lonely for what was his, for what was familiar, he returned home again to Cochin, both different and yet the same. His family thought they had lost him forever, and they welcomed him back with joy, the eldest son of an eldest son. And soon he married and had children, and when his father was gone he took over control of the business. And as his family grew he told his sons and daughters the stories and teachings he had learned from that teacher, weaving them into the stories of their own people. And he told the sailors of his people those stories too, and they took them back to their homeland, along with spices and cloth and precious stones. Soon his grandchildren would be old enough for him to tell them those stories, of the teacher in the mountains who had awakened from illusion. But now word had come to him that his teacher was dead, and then two kinds of death began to weave themselves together for him, two stories. Of temple gone, and teacher gone.

Sitting by the water he could picture the forest clearing, could see the master's elder disciples beating on small drums, the rest of the disciples repeating a chant, the chant they chanted whenever one of their circle had gone. Eliezer sat there, repeating it softly to himself. He could picture the teacher's body wrapped in cloth, covered with flowers, silent and still on its funeral pyre, and he could see the flames rising up like vertical waves of searing gold. He could smell the smell of incense and burning flesh. And he thought of that temple in his homeland that he had never seen, and he imagined its priests and its prophets. He knew their words. He knew their stories, he had read the scrolls. Isaiah, Jeremiah, Amos and Micah and a woman called Huldah. Yes, he knew the stories, he had read them, haltingly, parroting back to his grand-father the stories he told him. "In the beginning Agni created . . . " Grandfather's hand on his wrist, "Not Agni! Adonai, Our Lord. Adonai created the heavens and the earth." Repeated, corrected, all of those stories. The beautiful garden, the very first man, the magic tree, the big boat and the flood. The tower. The ancestor who discovered the one God. And that temple, that great temple, built by the king who had first sent his ancestors to this land, that great temple itself going up in an ocean of vertical flames.

. The monkeys began to shout, to leap from tree to tree, wildly, so that a green rain was falling on them. But the monks kept chanting, around the body of their teacher, the awakened one, the one who sat under a tree alone until he became enlightened. And Eliezer kept swaying, back and forth, back and forth between Co-chin and Kusinara, where the teacher was gone.

And then he turned his back on the sea, recalling an earlier time, the day that one of the traders who worked for his family had told him for the first time about a new kind of teacher, about a man who sat beneath a tree until he realized everything that there was to know. Those stories excited him. And he brought them to his father. "Did you hear? About the teacher in the mountains. Who sits under a tree." But his father had no time for stories. He was running the family's business, with its ships and its goods and its sailors. "Did you hear, Grandfather, about the teacher who sits in the mountains under a tree?" But his grandfather was too old, his eyes too clouded with other stories. "Did you hear, Mother, about the teacher in the north? I want to go and hear him." But his mother scolded him. "We have our own stories." And she shooed him away. She had too many things to do. And his sisters and his brothers did not care.

The wind rustled the leaves above his head, banyan and mango and jujube, each one speaking in its own language. And the tall line of palms behind the house, fronds clattering in conversation, as a shiny dark fly buzzed around him. He waved it off. And then the air was still, and he could hear clearly the sounds of Hebrew carried to him, a wailing chant, and then the wind turned, and it was gone. Then a serpent of smoke from the altar whipped past him and raced toward the sea, another sacrifice, a goat, a lamb. The smell of burning flesh, of incense, his family's incense. Gone.

He was smiling.

Looking at Texts, Again and Again, in This New Era

RECORDED BY PROFESSOR LAILAH DEVORAH KAFEH OF
HEBREW UNIVERSITY, ANTARCTICA CITY

WE SPEND THE MORNING of our first day together by simply reading and rereading familiar passages, in Hebrew as well as in Spanish, English, French, Yiddish, Arabic, Russian, Swahili, Farsi, Mandarin, and Ladino, seeking to hear and understand them in deep new ways. Sitting in sealed quarters, writing on devices that were shielded from the Outernet, we felt, most of us agreed, like ancient scribes sitting in exile in the time just after the destruction of the Second Temple, hoping to preserve what we remembered of our sacred scrolls, so that we could preserve our stories and traditions and be able to pass them on to our descendants.

These are the texts that we were invited to explore by Rabbi Sara-Rosa:

Exodus 20:8–11—*Remember the Sabbath day, to keep it holy. Six days you shall labor, and do all your work, but the seventh day is a Sabbath to YHWH your God. On it you shall not do any work, you, or your son, or your daughter, your male servant, or your female servant, or your livestock, or the stranger who is within your gates. For in six days YHWH made heaven and earth, the sea, and all that is in them, and rested on the seventh day. Therefore YHWH blessed the Sabbath day and made it holy.*

Deuteronomy 5:12–15–*Observe the Sabbath day, to keep it holy, as YHWH your God commanded you. Six days you shall labor and do all your work, but the seventh day is a Sabbath to YHWH your God. On it you shall not do any work, you or your son or your daughter or your male servant or your female servant, or your ox or your donkey or any of your livestock, or the stranger who is within your gates, that your male servant and your female servant may rest as well as you. You shall remember that you were a slave in the land of Egypt, and YHWH your God brought you out from there with a mighty hand and an outstretched arm. Therefore YHWH your God commanded you to keep the Sabbath day.*

Exodus 31:12–17–*And YHWH spoke to Moses, saying: 'You shall keep My Sabbaths, for it is a sign between Me and you through-out your generations, that you may know that I am YHWH who sanctifies you. You shall keep the Sabbath therefore, for it is holy unto you; every one that profanes it shall be put to death; for whosoever does any work, that soul shall be cut off from among his people. Six days shall work be done; but the seventh day is a Sabbath of solemn rest, holy to YHWH; whosoever does any work in the Sabbath day, he shall surely be put to death. The children of Israel shall keep the Sabbath, and observe the Sabbath throughout their generations, for a perpetual covenant. It is a sign between Me and the children of Israel for ever; for in six days YHWH made heaven and earth, and on the seventh day He ceased from work and rested.*

We also looked at two additional core texts, those which gave our ancestors the conceptual foundation for the practice of "Pi-kuach Nefesh," the mandate to violate Sabbath restrictions in order to save a life, which were written about in the *Mishnah* and the commentaries upon it:

Leviticus 18:5–*You shall keep my statutes and my rules; if a person does them, he shall live by them: I am YHWH.*

Ezekiel 20:11–*And I gave them my statutes, and showed them my judgments, which if a man do, he shall even live in them.*

Rabbi Sinfa Rosa of San Salvador reminded us of the words of the 20th century rabbi Abraham Joshua Heschel, who likened the Sabbath to a palace in time rather than in space. And Professor Dan Strober of Portland reminded us of the famous words of Ahad Ha'am, that more than the Jews keeping the Sabbath, the Sabbath has kept the Jews.

With those texts echoing in the room, we deepened our conversation into the leading question that Rabbi Sara-Rosa had presented us with:

How do we observe the Sabbath in a time when every single day is life-threatening and dangerous?

Rabbi Daniel of Vietnam said, "In such a time it is a mitzvah of its own to violate the Sabbath. Because the air we breathe is deadly and we must act at every moment to keep the holy spark in us alive, whatever it takes."

Reb Malcolm Italia of the Denver Yeshiva agreed with him, saying, "Even though it seems as if the world is dying, we must live, must do all we can to keep ourselves and our children and those around us alive."

Maggid Hanna Rose Tong said, "In such a dangerous time, when the norms of our ancestors for thousands of years have been violated, by greed and cruelty and corruption, I believe that it's more important than ever to hold onto the very basic rules and regulations that govern Shabbat observance."

Hazzan Dina Yankelovich said, "If it's Shabbat morning and a fire is burning nearby then we must put it out, and thus, when it is Shabbat morning and the world around us is going up in flames, we must put out those flames."

Rabbi Tina-Rob Cohen said, "Speaking in metaphoric language in such times is itself inflammatory. Now, every single word we speak must be carefully chosen to do the work of healing."

Reb Malcolm agreed with her, saying, "Now more than ever every single thought we think and every single act we do must be held to be an act of Tikkun Olam."

Professor Trent Lefkowitz said, "What is the value of holding such thoughts, in a time when, if there is a God, It must surely have abandoned us?"

Rabbah Sofie Allura said, "No. That's not our way, to fall into despair like that about the nature of Goddix. We must remember the old Talmudic story in *Bava Metzia* about Rabbi Eliezer and his decision on whether or not a particular oven was kosher. When all the other sages disagreed with him he said, "If Halachah agrees with me, let that carob tree outside the window prove it," and the tree moved. Still the others didn't agree with him, not when at his command a stream reversed itself or when the walls of their House of Study began to bend. And when a voice from heaven announced that Eliezer was right, Rabbi Joshua reminded the gathering of the words from Deuteronomy 30:12 that the Torah is not in the heavens. And another sage quoted Exodus 23:2 that we must decide according to the majority. But none of that is my point. My point is the end of the story, when Rabbi Nathan runs into Elijah the Prophet on the way home and asks him what God's reaction was to the day's events and Elijah tells him that God was laughing at the outcome, saying, "My children have defeated me, my children have defeated me."

Rabbi Yonah Klein asked, "I'm sorry, but what is your point?"

Rabbah Sofie answered, "That whether or not Goddix has abandoned us, or even if Goddix exists is not important in this conversation. What's important is the laws around Shabbat that were given to us long ago, and what's important is how we interpret them in a time when it seems as if the world is coming to an end."

Maggidah Regina Kohen responded, "The answer to that question is clear. Not working on Shabbat is no longer relevant."

Reb Peninah Jones shouted, "That is not an appropriate response. Pikuach Nefesh is and must always be situational. We cannot rescind or eliminate mitzvot. We can only work with them."

Rabbi Kronenberg agreed.

Rabbi Steinfield agreed.

Professor Strober agreed.

Doctor Haverford agreed.

Rabbi Abouav agreed.

Rabbi Rodrigawitz agreed.

Hazzanit Ruthie Gordon said, "This conversation has defeated me. This conversation has defeated me."

Reb Tarkoman turned to her in fury. "How dare you appropriate those words!"

Rabbi Abouav said, "One made in the image of God—can speak for God."

Fragment 9

[...]

were all gathered together in Seventh Heaven. And God said to them, "I know that most of you did not approve of My creation of human beings, and looking back on it, I probably should have paid more attention to your thoughtful, if at times outraged and perhaps envious critique."

There was a great hush in the hall. Some of the angels nodded, others bowed their heads. Some smiled, one laughed out loud, and a few began to weep soft opalescent tears.

God nodded, solemnly, and said, "Now, here we are at the end of the eighth day of My creation. What a very long day, for those mortal humans, and what a singular day for us here. As we approach day nine it occurs to Me that it's been quite a while since I've tried something new."

That hush turned into a silence never heard before in heaven. A silence so deep that if angels had pumping hearts instead of shining ones–you could have heard them all beating.

God continued. "I've considered all sorts of things. And what I finally decided is that I want to do some renovating. Not down there, although I admit that it needs it, but up here. Because I find that I need, and I think that we all need, some more elbow room, wing room. So what I'm going to do is to create an Eighth Heaven.

[...]

Late October in Eden Gardens

BY TOBIAS THE MAGGID OF THE SUBWAYS

THE THREE OF THEM crossed the lobby and stopped to look at the four-story-high atrium, filled with trees and caged songbirds, a waterfall cascading down the far wall.

"Oh Mom. It's so beautiful. You really picked a perfect place."

The bellhop was used to people stopping to take in the view, and she paused discretely behind them.

"Thanks, Sweetheart," Innette said, one arm around her daughter Selda, the other resting lightly on her granddaughter Rebecca's shoulder.

"It's prettier than the pictures, Gran."

"I think we're going to have a grand week, girls." Having said that, Innette turned to the bellhop, who slipped in front of them and led them around the atrium toward a bank of elevators. They zipped up to the top floor, and she led them to their suite, a large sitting room that looked out on a terrace, with three bedrooms down a short hallway.

Rebecca was excited. Except for visiting her other grandmother twice a year, this was her first big vacation. She and her mother had gone away from time to time on weekends, sharing a motel room, but she was especially excited about having her own room for the first time in a big fancy resort. Selda had been nervous about that, about the extra expense, and had tried to talk her mother out of it. But Innette reminded her that her insurance paid for eighty percent of it and that she'd been saving up for years to do this trip perfectly–and that not only did she want Selda to have her own room, but she wanted her to be able to pick it out. So they'd gone to the resort's z-site and explored all the available suites until Selda found one she liked, with a terrace and all the bedrooms looking out on the waterfall, and a wonderful view through the dome, out to the rolling desert hills beyond it.

Innette tipped the bellhop and she left them, after showing them where the waterbar was and pointing out the info-cube that would tell them everything they might want to know about Eden Gardens. She reminded them that their personal activities coordinator would come to see them the next morning, that dinner was served from five to eight and that they had the whole day to settle in and explore.

Selda and Innette stood at the end of the hall watching Rebecca as she raced from bedroom to bedroom, calling out as she darted in and out of each, "This is yours Mommy. This is yours Gran. And this one is mine." Mine was the room at the far end of the hall, the smallest, but the only one with windows on two walls, looking out on the waterfall from one side and through the atrium to the dusty hills outside the dome on the other.

Innette and Selda followed Rebecca, carrying all of their bags, putting them in their own rooms and then delivering Rebecca's to hers. Rebecca kept calling for them. "Mommy, Gran, come quickly. You have to see this." The two adults arrived, smiling, and joined Rebecca, who was standing in front of the floor-to-ceiling window. Below them, in the atrium, a peacock was strutting about, under the trees. Innette and Selda were just as amazed as Rebecca was, for there were very few peacocks left in the world, and neither of them had ever seen one before. They came up behind Rebecca and put their hands on her shoulders, and all three gasped when a moment later the bird turned and snapped open its fan. A flash of turquoise, shimmering, golden, fluttering, huge.

"Oh my!" Innette said, startled.

"Wow!" said Selda.

"Diggers!" Rebecca added, laughing. "Do you think it did it for us?" Innette leaned over and kissed her only grandchild on the top of her head.

"Of course he did, Rebecca," who ran to her suitcase, flipped open the locks, pulled out her clothing and tossed it on the bed. As her mother and grandmother watched she systematically carried everything over to the dresser and closet, and started to put all of her things away, beginning with her underwear, socks, shirts, and air-fixes in the dresser drawers.

"I didn't teach her to do that," Selda said to her mother, as they watched her. Innette, remembering what a slob Selda had been as a child, laughed.

"And when I'm done we can all go swimming," Rebecca said, looking up at them. "There are four pools. We can try them all."

"Let's all unpack first, Honey. And maybe Grandma wants to rest for a while. We had a long trip and maybe she's tired."

"Not a chance," Innette said. "Besides, I don't want to miss a single minute of fun. But how about some lunch first?"

"We can eat at the Tel Aviv Café, the Jerusalem Veranda, the Jericho Grill, or at the Haifa Terrace," Rebecca rattled off, names that meant almost nothing to her.

"I see we won't have to use the info-cube."

"Oh no. I know everything," Rebecca announced, as she hung up two body-suits in the closet, a fancy one and one to go hiking in.

"I told her not to bring them both," Selda said to her mother, "but she insisted."

"Well, we ought to go hiking one day, and you never can tell when you might want to look nice." An adoring grandmother, anything that Rebecca did was all right with her.

"Well hurry up, you two. Get unpacked and let's go eat. Then, we can go swimming. I want to try the heart-shaped pool up on the roof first."

Half an hour later, after Selda had changed and unpacked, after Innette had taken the little nap she said she didn't need, the three of them were sitting at a small round table at the Tel Aviv

Café, at the far end of the atrium, just beside the waterfall. The café was crowded, and Selda couldn't help but notice the other families gathered there, and a few single people, and found herself staring at the eldest member at each table. Everyone seemed to be having a good time, and she wondered if she were the only one who felt a little bit nervous, anxious, in fact fearful about being there. Her mother was her usual blustery self, and Rebecca seemed to be having the time of her life. There was an artificial breeze, and every few minutes a soft spray would waft over their table, catching on skin, sparkling on eyelashes. Rebecca had been to several real waterfalls before, but always wearing a body-suit and air-fix. She'd seen the spray on the visor of her fix, but never felt it before. Each time it blew over them she would lick the spray off her face, laughing.

As soon as they'd ordered, Rebecca turned the compu-screen that was their tabletop from menu-function to activities-function, and between bites of her lunch she was showing her mother and grandmother the different trails she thought they ought to explore. "This one goes up to some old Indian ruins, and this one goes to an old cowboy ghost town," she said, pointing to the colored trails. "But Mommy, you promised I could get a new air-fix, and I saw some zadd ones in the gift shop."

"Rebecca, when did you manage to do that?" her grandmother asked, a half a smile on his face.

"When you and Mommy were checking in. They had two nice ones. A blue one with yellow spots all over it. And another one that looked like a bird. It was all shiny and would go with my new body-suit."

"We can look at them after lunch."

Selda reached a hand across the table and put it on her mother's forearm. "Mom, don't spoil her."

"Spoil her? I just want to make her happy. Besides . . . "

Selda interrupted her.

"If you insist."

So they finished their lunches, and while Selda sat by one of the pools, Innette and Rebecca went off to the gift shop, and came back ten minutes later with Rebecca wearing the bird fix.

"It's beautiful Honey. But you really shouldn't have, Mom."

"Come on. That's what this time is for. To have fun and enjoy ourselves. Besides, we want our big girl to be the best dressed hiker when we go out tomorrow."

"To the ruins. I've never seen real ruins before. Just those hologram ones they have at the Natural History Museum."

"It's a deal. We can go right after breakfast."

"Don't forget that the coordinator will be coming in the morning, Mom. And then the doctor."

"I haven't forgotten. We can go right after that." So they spent the rest of the day exploring every enclosed corner of Eden Gardens that Rebecca led them to. Through the health spa and the bowling alley, the holovision center, the music-listening rooms, and all four pools. They ate dinner in their suite. Rebecca had never had room service before and decided that when she grew up she wanted to be a hospitality worker in a resort and order room service for every single meal. And she loved being tucked in by her mother and her grandmother, who read to her till she fell asleep, from her favorite bedtime reading, a book about the planets in our solar system.

Rebecca was up first, checking out the breakfast menu in the sitting room when the door flashed and announced that their activities coordinator was there. Rebecca beeped her in and was delighted when Ronit said, "You must be Rebecca." She let Ronit know that her mother and grandmother were still asleep and offered to wake them. But Ronit said it was fine with her, to let them sleep awhile, that it would give the two of them a chance to talk.

"How do you like it here so far?"

"It's great. After room service and after you go, Gran and me are going for a hike. Out to the ruins."

"How do you feel about being here?"

"I'm really happy for us and happy for Gran. She says she's been planning for this vacation for almost her whole entire life."

"Then you know what's going to happen?"

"Sure. If you read up on me and on Gran then you should know that on a planet of over 15 billion people, taking responsibility for your life is an essential requirement for all world citizens."

Ronit laughed. "That's from one of your grandmother's talks, isn't it?"

Rebecca nodded. "I've heard them all. Sometimes she practices on me, on the View-screen, before she goes to give another talk."

Just then, awakened by the sound of them talking, Innette came out of her room, in a long blue bathrobe. Ronit introduced herself and Innette joined them on the couch.

"Good morning Senator Goldberg-Kwan."

"Oh, just call me Innette. Everyone does."

"I've read through your charts, Innette, and of course I know all about your career. We're all so very honored and pleased and proud to have you here with us at Eden. Your work has made such a difference in the world."

Rebecca popped in with, "Gran's work was all about *tikkun olam*! Which is why she picked it here and not anywhere else," just as her mother staggered in, rubbing her eyes, half awake, and sat on a chair off to the side, longing for a cup of coffee.

"You are so right, Rebecca. And now that your mother is here, it's time to talk with all of you about this wonderful week that your grandmother selected for the three of you to share. We've arranged for every meal that you've asked for, Innette. We've also arranged for a chamber group to be flown in, to play the Bach concert you z-mailed me about. And lastly, our on-staff videographers will be filming every moment of this special week for the two of you to treasure, Rebecca and Selda."

Selda looked away and said nothing. Rebecca had a few questions about the video, and about the clothes she'd brought with her. Ronit told her that there were several boutiques in Eden if she wanted or needed anything special, and said that she'd be happy to go shopping with her once the staff doctor and his staff arrived. Then she turned back to Innette. "Frankly, we're all a little bit embarrassed, because you've written so much on this subject, and we've all heard so many of your lectures, that we don't have to ask you the battery of questions that we ask all of our other new guests. We know exactly what you want, and we want to let you know that everything will proceed as you wanted, down to the potted lily-of-the-valley plants at the departure ceremony. We found a man in New Zealand with an extensive greenhouse, whose specialty is breeding heirloom plants from North America."

Innette thanked her, and added, "You have all been so wonderful. This is exactly how I want to spend my last week. And who I want to spend it with–all of you included."

On Observing the 6th of Av

BY RABBI RUFUS ANNE GREENBLATT

SESSION RECORDER

BELOW YOU WILL FIND a brief description of conversations we had in closed sessions about the celebration of the 6th of Av that was originally created by Andrew Elias Ramer, the world's first interfaith maggid, in the early years of the 21st century.

It was on the 6th day of the month of Av in 5416, which was July 27th 1656, that Baruch de Espinosa, the philosopher known to us as Benedict Spinoza, was excommunicated by the Amsterdam Portuguese Jewish community, for what they defined as his "evil opinions and acts," that date chosen deliberately, three days before the 9th of Av, the anniversary of the destruction of the first and second temples. We know that 21st century Maggid Ramer observed the day by reading Spinoza and eating something treif at every meal, which he did not do otherwise, and we know that slowly, after his death, the celebration began to be observed by others around the world.

Our discussions were heated and long, as several of the attendees shun the festival while others celebrate it with varying degrees of observance, including liturgical innovations and all-night study sessions. Several of our members defended the observance, citing its inclusivity as an important contribution to global Jewry, bridging the often-wide gulf between secular or cultural Jews and religious Jews, and bridging the gulf between religious and observant Jews of various denominations and movements. Maggid Ramer's descendant, the noted rabbi and author, said, "Even if we as a collective choose to reject the day, my family, my community, and I will continue to observe it." While a number of our other members observe the day as Ramer created it, in celebration of Spinoza, who has been called both "the first secular Jew" and "the first secular human being," others were horrified by the violation of Torah prohibitions, and by the embrace of a man who seems to have rejected the Jewish community of his time and place as much as it rejected him.

We debated in closed meetings for six days and finally held a vote on the following resolution, which we crafted for the wider convocation:

> We in council recommend with full regard to the range of individual and community practices, from celebratory to contemptuous, that in recognition of the profound contributions of Baruch Spinoza to the values of conscience we all uphold, that all surviving Jewish communities adopt and adapt as suits them a celebration of Spinoza Day, to be held each year on the 6th of Av.

Our resolution was passed twenty-eight to eleven, with two abstentions.

The Five Books of Mona

In Six Voices & One Narrator

BY LYDIA NAKAMURA RAMER

Table of Concepts:
Time:
The past
Plot:
Entirely derivative
Settings:
The slender island of Manhattan
A few selected vacation spots
The majestic borough of Brooklyn
The magnificent city of Oakland
Several exotic dream locations
Characters:
Mona–our protagonist
Leopold–her late father
Jivin–her ex-husband
Chantal–their older twin daughter, named Carlos at birth
Leticia–their younger twin daughter, by seven minutes
Eduardo–Mona's former boss and intermittent beau
Theme:
This is a tale of Memory, Life, Death, and Family–in other words, an ordinary narrative of moderate length, perhaps a novel

Chapter one: *Bereishit*–In a beginning

1 The room was a total mess. She knew it, lying beneath and entangled in her grandmother Arnetta's crazy-quilt, in total darkness. Clothing strewn all over the floor, shoes, socks, and piles of books, magazines, newspapers, littering every surface and spreading out on the known but invisible floor. But as Mona turned over in bed, yawned, sighed, reached for the light, flipped it on, even the chaos of her room looked good to her, in the rose-purple glow of the full-spectrum light bulb she'd bought the day before in her favorite health food store on Broadway.

2 Peeling back the purple, blue, and aqua quilt, its squares a riot of differing patterns, some bold and some subtle and with everything in between, and pushing it aside, Mona slid out of bed, swinging her feet onto the dark blue shag rug.

3 It was suddenly cold, and she did not like the cold. But she did like the feel of solid floor beneath her as she slipped into her slippers and stood, stretched, yawned again and, thinking of coffee, she slid her gnarled feet into her slippers, went into the bathroom, and filled up the large tin watering can that always reminded her of a crane, with its long angled spout. Her room was a jungle, of potted plants and hanging plants, ficus, geranium, philodendron, a snake plant, in terra cotta pots on the floor, windowsills, and the tops of every bookcase, of which there were several.

4 Plants watered, Mona reached for the bathrobe she'd tossed on the chair by the bed the night before, an opulent robe, fancier than anything she'd had before. Mona found an ad for it in a catalog at the dentist, took it home, saved it for months, and then sent for it as a present for herself, for her fiftieth birthday. Every time she put it on she smiled. It was silk, the right half brilliant yellow, covered with red scattered suns, round, eight rays shooting out from each one. The left side was indigo, covered with silver crescent moons and a spray of countless shining stars.

5 Opening her bedroom door, Mona walked up the stairs to the living room where she took off the cover draped over the large cage in which her three canaries, Stella, Bella, and Irving began to hop from perch to perch, singing. Mona whistled back at them and turned to her fish tank, her eyes met by darting silver, shimmering orange, sliding reds, greens, all of which rose to the surface as she sprinkled their food from a large white container with circling koi on it. The birds singing, the fish feeding, Mona headed down the hall to the kitchen.

6 Hearing her approaching footsteps, Mona's old arthritic golden retriever Panther pushed herself up from her padded bed in the corner next to the refrigerator and, with nails scraping on the linoleum, headed toward Mona, who leaned down to greet her, rubbing her head, stroking her back. After feeding her, Mona opened the back door to let in her cats, Vicky and Raul, who darted in, swirled around her legs, rubbing against her, purring with delight as she headed toward the canister on the counter which held their food. Three beasts slurping and inhaling around her, she filled and turned on the coffee maker, eyes looking back and forth from the window over the sink to her garden, and to the picture of her children when they were little, the twins, which hung on the wall to her left. Her pride and joy, even before her magnificent garden, Mona smiled with contentment as she counted the many blessings of her life.

7 It was Saturday, the start of a holiday weekend. Filling a mug with coffee and heading out into the garden, Mona took a seat beneath her favorite

[...]

. . . the diner was filled with revelers, back from the annual Thanksgiving Day Parade. Many were in costumes ranging from superheroes to high drag to cowboy leather, and one group staggered in in rainbow colors, clearly intoxicated or otherwise mind-altered, carrying on their shoulders a very large wobbly piñata in the shape of a golden giraffe. Mona, sitting on the upper balcony trying to read the morning paper . . .

[. . .]
hot
. . . in a thunderous voice . . .

[. . .]

. . . long snaking strands of Mardi Gras beads hanging from his neck, the Hollywood sign, its gigantic letters illuminated behind him, shining out in the bakingly hot starless night. Lupi was carrying a book of some kind. Perry was waving a yellow rubber chicken, or was it a pig? Later, no one could remember. Claudia was reciting a line from the movie that she'd found compelling, while Letitia was trying to pick up a wireless line to call . . .

[. . .]

. . . not written in stone," she said, staring out at the . . .

[. . .]

Fragment 10

[...]

. . . and then God sent hosts of angels to the planet Quingi, where they have seven genders. And the angels appeared to all of them in midst of a bright golden light and said to them, all speaking together in one loud voice, "Now. Today . . .

[...]

To each gender a corps of angels was dispatched, each according to their body, and the light that they gave off was blinding. And the prophet Nus'Mai'Aht said to the worshippers gathered around the steps to the temple, "Oh you of bright hopes. Bring to the altar your . . .

[...]

. . . spread their wings as the sovereign of Inzak, on bended knee, moved close to the fiery altar and begged them for their teachings. And all assembled fell to their knees, old and young, and the angels rose up in the air above the kneeling throng, and they divided themselves into seven choruses, one for each of the seven genders, and to each gender they raised up an image of a seven-faced God, seated on a golden throne. And the voices of the angels sounded like . . .

[...]

The Next Step

By Rabbi Sandro Meller

God summoned all six hundred and fourteen octillion of us angels to heaven. He had never done that before. The angelic amphitheatre in sixth heaven had to be vastly enlarged. Yes, God summoned all of us to heaven at the same time and said to us, from the vast luminous throne He was seated in, high up on stage, "Welcome My darlings. Settle in. Relax. It's wonderful to see all of you sitting here together." At God's suggestion we all looked around, and it really was an amazing sight.

Then God went on. "I've invited you here because I have something important to say to all of you."

We paused, relaxed and utterly intrigued.

God went on, smiling warmly, and said to the gathered throng, "This is something that I've been thinking about for a very long time. And as it concerns you all, I wanted all of you to hear the news from Me directly, in the same place and at the very same time." God smiled, paused, and tenderly looked around at all of us, one by one at the exact same time, as only God can do, and then said, with a mixture of calmness and authority in His loving voice, "I have decided–to retire."

"What?!!!" we all shouted, rising to our feet. "That's impossible. How can you retire? You're the sole Creator and Sustainer of all that is!"

God smiled at us and said, "So you agree, then, that I am Omniscient, Omnipresent, and Omnipotent?"

How could we not shout out at once, all in one voice again, "Of course we do. It's the truth!"

To which God replied. "Good. Very good."

We all sat back down, wings wrapped round ourselves, trembling, wondering what was about to come next.

Then God said, "As you all agree with Me about the truth of My very nature, you will surely understand that it's entirely within My power as God–to do anything that I want. And I want to retire."

Terror and amazement raced through heaven as we sank back into our seats, considering the unimaginable prospect.

God went on. "This is something that I've been thinking about for a very long time. And I have taken all the necessary steps to insure a smooth transition."

"Transition?" We all rose up in our seats again, utterly puzzled.

"Yes. Transition." God paused here and looked around the amphitheatre again, taking in each and every single one of us, inviting us to settle back down in our seats. Then He continued. "Darlings, I'd like you all to meet someone."

We rose up from our seats again as an elegant woman with short-cropped gray hair, in a black sleeveless cocktail dress, and a string of pearls around her neck, wearing spiked black satin high heels, walked across the vast shining stage toward God's exalted throne. As she approached, a second throne appeared beside it. The two smiled at each other, the exact same smile on two different faces, as He turned to us and said, "Darlings, I'd like you all to meet–my sister."

"Sister??!!" Puzzled, amazed, shocked, horrified, delighted, curious, and intrigued, we sat with wings aflutter in our comfortable seats.

She nodded and smiled, and settling into Her own throne, She took in all of us in just the way that He always had.

Then He went on. "All will be well, My darlings," and He proceeded to answer our most burning unvoiced questions.

"No. She did not exist before. Yes, She is all that you think She is. And no, She was not hidden away in the wings, so to speak."

We all laughed.

"But if you all agree, as you will have to, that I am utterly omniscient, omnipresent, and omnipotent, then one of the things that I as God can do–is to create for Myself–a sister. So, I did. And another thing that I can do–is retire. But I want to assure you that each and every single one of you, and all of the universe too, will be in good hands. Very good hands."

Having said that, God and His Sister joined hands, smiling, and the vast amphitheatre was filled with golden light. And we noticed that Her high spiked heels had turned into a pair of turquoise tennis shoes, just as, with a sudden burst of diamond-bright light–God utterly vanished, throne and all, leaving only His Sister, seated comfortably in a high exalted throne up on the stage.

"Welcome," She said to all of us, in a warm rich caring voice, and we all relaxed, knowing that everything was indeed going to be all right.

Fragment 11

[...]

    ... and spring comes to Hell once every ten thousand Earth years. Everyone looks forward to it, humans and angels alike. Everything stops, for it's the time when patients–we used to call them sinners, then prisoners–meet with their rehabilitation counselors–we used to call them demons and then we called them guards–to determine their future treatment. For some it's more time in rehab, and for others, it's release to other departments, up to heaven for some and back to Earth for others.

    Personally, I love it when spring arrives. Not just the feeling of lightness in the air, but the sense of hope and renewal. Winter is bleak here, frigid for more than a thousand Earth years. Summer is infernal, autumn so depressing, but spring, spring is joyous. I know that all of us angels anticipate it. And over the eons spring has been a time of hope for everyone, as we watched humanity evolve and grow, which is why this last spring was so very difficult. We thought that everything was going according to plan, that consciousness and compassion were continuing to grow, as they had been, ever since the last Ice Age. That seemed to be the trend, following The Boss's master plan. But something happened in the last two thousand or so Earth years. A shift. A circling backward. Not to what was, not to the same old dualities and the ways that they distorted the sacred purpose of incarnation–which is the soul's opportunity to learn and grow. No. People in some ways grew wiser and wiser, at the very same time as their wrongdoings–we used to call them sins–grew more and more dangerous, not just against other human beings and other life forms, but increasingly against the planet itself.

We angels held a conference fifteen hundred Earth years ago. I was invited to be a presenter, along with Auriel and Nicanor and . . . . . . [. . .]

On Children

RECORDED BY KOHENET RIVKA DARDASHTI

RABBI SAM ALKALAI SAID, "Sara-Rosa invited us to talk about the first commandment given to us in the Torah, to be fruitful and multiply."

Rabbah Channah bat Simcha said, "That commandment is essential in such trying times. We must survive."

Doctor Kory Winestsky said, "There is no commandment to survive, just to live, which isn't the same thing."

Reb Carlos Morena said, "Abraham was forbidden to murder his son. We must do all that we can do to preserve humanity."

Professor Charlie Kaplan asked, "Why? I think this planet will be better off without us."

Rabbi Ethel Greenblat said, "Abraham not killing Isaac at God's command didn't stop Jephthah the Judge from sacrificing his nameless daughter."

Cantor Carlotta Tunney said, "You're confusing us. We aren't murdering anyone."

Rabbi Dolores Weingarten said, "I follow you, Cantor. But it seems to me that by our continued involvement in the structures of evil that are running the world–that we *are* killing our children!"

Professor Harmony Rothschild said, "It isn't just our children. This is worse than the story of Noah, for in our time there's a good chance that NO living beings will survive."

Doctor Ezra Greenberg said, "And where is God in all of this?"

Rabbi Harold Blumberg said, "Auschwitz. Biafra. Rwanda. Bosnia. Syria. Texas. Djakarta."

Hazzan Tillie Aptos said, "This conversation is essential, but what troubles me is that between rising infertility and the continued rise of the oceans, the demise of the bees and many other pollinating species, all of life is in danger, and the commandment to each of us to reproduce seems less to me a requirement than an impossibility. My partner and I have been trying to have children for years. His sperm are nearly nonexistent and my eggs are decaying at a rapid rate. We have tried every treatment, and the biological urge to have children of our own, implanted in us millions of years ago–is overpowering. To me that energy *is the living breath of God*. And feeling it . . . breaks my heart!"

Rabbi Carlos Wappner said, "Breath of God–or of the Devil?"

Rabbi Aptos replied, "Do we really think like that?"

Rabbi Blumberg said, "Does it even matter what we think anymore? Everyone and everything is dying."

Rabbah bat Simcha said, with tears in her eyes, "After three miscarriages in my first trimester, I never conceived again, despite every known and available treatment. My wife and I often say that we feel like Adam and Eve, thrust out of the Garden of Eden. Only, their lives of pleasure and parenthood began after the expulsion, while ours have ended."

Rabbi Anna Fortuni said, "I pray that Shechinah carry us all aloft on Her shining wings, to a world of joy and safety, of beauty and delight. And I invite us all to say Kaddish now, for ourselves, each other, and for the rest of this world."

Fragment 12

Ark-less

After the cows were gone
And the sheep were gone
The chickens, the ducks,
Even geese were gone . . .
We began to eat
Our last surviving pets.

The End

(PERHAPS THE VERY END)

We clasp the hands of those that go before us,
And the hands of those who come after us.
We enter the little circle of each other's arms
And the larger circle of lovers,
Whose hands are joined in a dance
And the larger circle of all creatures
Passing in and out of life
Who move also in a dance
To music so subtle and vast that no ear hears it
Except in fragments.

Wendell Berry

Afterword

VERTIGINOUS AND DOWN TO earth, poetic and crass, ancient and futuristic—all the adjectives of extremes throw sparks of light on the Brooklyn Talmud but do not describe it. Just like the Talmud of old, it has structure but no boundaries. You may skip from a wilted flower in a mayonnaise jar to a wireless text from the Messiah in Urdu in the space of a page. Rabbi Tarfon's wisdom gives way to Porky the Pig. This is not your grandfather's Talmud. Or even yours, yet.

But as the quota of irreverence is high, the undercurrent of piety is steady and true. This is the Talmud in a postmodern blender and what comes out is fantastical, weird, wise and altogether unexpected. If Blade Runner met Babylonia met Brooklyn, Andrew Ramer would be the chronicler of their clash. In fact, he is both the creator and the chronicler.

The great Canadian novelist Robertson Davies said the writer needs but one thing—the wand of the enchanter. Here is enchantment to disturb the traditionalist (I certainly read it disturbed), to provoke, to inspire, to instruct and to amuse. Just like the original Talmud. Except completely different. The hand of an unexpected future has lain this hybrid on our unsuspecting laps. Go back and learn again.

Rabbi David Wolpe
Sinai Temple, Los Angeles
author of *David: The Divided Heart*

Notes

Books for me grow out of the marriage of two things: inspiration—and regret. After *Queering the Text* was published I was annoyed with myself that I hadn't included a section about Jewish lesbians reading Sappho in ancient Alexandria, to go just before the stories about gay men in medieval Spain. Filled with divine inspiration (please note that I did not say Divine inspiration) I wrote a story about just such women for my next book, *Torah Told Different.* But after that book was published I found myself living with a body-aching despair that in the story set in Cordoba I hadn't made the rabbi a woman. That lingering regret led me on a journey of rectification in my next book, *Deathless,* whose central character Serach isn't a rabbi but a three thousand year old Hebrew woman sage. But after *Deathless* was published and I read the bound version for the first time, I was once again filled with regret—that I had given Hebrew names to the Persian rabbi and his wife who befriended Serach and not Persian ones. Rabbi Sara-Rosa's Persian ancestry on her father's side is my best attempt to heal that lingering sorrow.

Queering the Text, Torah Told Different, and *Deathless* all look out from imagined pasts into altered presents, so it's no surprise that my Jewish muses would eventually inspire me to leap into two time frames of an imaginary and dystopian future in this book. Once the idea was conceived—of a noted woman rabbi of Persian descent in the future who would help me heal that foolish error in *Deathless*—I began to wander through old stories. As I read through them and started weaving them together with new stories, I came to understand that I had been working on this book all along, without any conscious idea of its existence—although I have often thought about the end of the world, which I explored in an unpublished book called *When People Still Lived on the Earth: or All of human history from beginning to end (and what happened afterward)*.

Inspiration and regret helped to birth a book that I hope you enjoyed, in spite of its depressing backdrop. And I hope too that the stories here do what a good story ought to do—invite and incite you to take action to make this world a better place.

"Good" was written at a poetry workshop led by marvelous Santa Cruz poet Ellen Bass, on Saturday the 11th of May 2003 at the San Francisco Public Library.

All of the Beata Roman stories were written for a tiny little book called *Future Dreaming* that I entirely incorporated into this one

The last line of "Speaking of our Forefathers" was inspired by the famous saying about Maimonides—"From Moses to Moses there was none like Moses."

"Vidui" was written for a mahzor for Congregation Sha'ar Zahav in San Francisco that never happened—or hasn't happened yet.

"A Night at the Movies" burst into my head fully grown while reading the chapter "Cecchino dei Bracchi" in Marguerite Yourcenar's amazing book *That Mighty Sculptor, Time,* while sitting on BART somewhere under the San Francisco Bay, the book a gift from Rabbi Tamara Eskenazi.

The two stories about Selda were written some years ago for an unpublished book, *Abducted by Aliens,* and I plucked them out of it and put them in here.

"A Tale for Tara Hannah Goldwasser, my Buddhist Grand-mother" was originally in *Torah Told Different* under a different title, but I removed it before the book went off to the editor and eventually put it here.

"Havdallah for a New Era" riffs on an alternate havdallah I spontaneously created at the Gay Spirituality Summit held at the Garrison Institute in New York in May of 2004, following a tradi-tional havdallah led by noted writer and teacher Jay Michaelson.

Versions of "A Counter-Dayenu" and "The Five Elders" were written for the Sha'ar Zahav *Pride Seder Haggadah* many years ago. The first one was used, the second one was not.

"I Dreamed of Graves" was inspired by a moving song by Jan Garrett titled "I Dreamed of Rain" that I learned from Mennonite pastor Ken Nafziger when we co-facilitated a peace conference at The Mountain Retreat Center in Highland, North Carolina, with the late wonderful Shelley Denham, during the summer of 2009, I think.

"The Ten Commandments of Global Healing" was written several years ago for the Joint Climate Action Committee of the First Mennonite Church of San Francisco and Congregation Sha'ar Zahav, which flourished for a while and then faded away, as do many such necessary groups.

The beginning of "Alternate Realities" was written for Tamara Eskenazi five or six years ago. The parts about Rabbi Avi de Leon and Professor Abu Levi were inspired by three exciting talks on the subject "Forgetting" given at the Magnes Museum in Berkeley by Professor Annette Yoshiko Reed of NYU in March of 2018.

I can't remember where the idea for "The Next Step" came from, but the notion of a second throne up in heaven comes from chapter seven in the book of *Daniel* in the Tanach, although I played around with it, which shouldn't surprise you.

I originally intended *The Five Books of Mona* to be a novel with 54 chapters, one for each of the Torah's weekly portions. After thinking about it for 20 years but having only written the very beginning, I realized that I'd run out of juice, that I wanted to leave writing midrash behind and just write pure fiction—and then I realized that the very few parts I'd already written belonged here, in a book with 66 fragments. You can figure out the gematria yourself.

It's horrifyingly eerie to have read through the typeset pages of this book in mid-November of 2018—while two huge fires are raging in California. The air quality is so hazardous that one can't go out without a breathing mask. The death toll mounts daily, the number of evacuated and homeless people grows, over 14,000 structures have been destroyed, and over 260,000 acres of land have burned. Horrifying eerie—because I thought I was writing about a time eighty years in the future.

Author Bio

ANDREW RAMER'S PARENTS GREW up around the corner from each other in Bensonhurst, Brooklyn, and he lived in Park Slope, Brooklyn for the longest he's lived anywhere (so far).

He is the author of four books of midrashim, beginning with *Queering the Text: Biblical, Medieval, and Modern Jewish Stories, Torah Told Different: Stories for a Pan/Poly/Post-Denominational Era,* and *Deathless: The Complete, Uncensored, Heartbreaking, and Amazing Autobiography of Serach bat Asher, the Oldest Woman in the World,* and ending with this book. Many of his prayers and blessings appear in the siddur of Congregation Sha'ar Zahav in San Francisco.

The world's first ordained interfaith maggid, he now lives in Oakland, California—but for him Brooklyn will always be the Promised Land.

www.andrewramer.com

Acknowledgements

I DON'T WRITE IN cafés, but even a book written at an old wooden desk in solitude is written in community. This book exists because of the warm loving support of my family who are friends and my friends who are family. You all know who you are! And with particular appreciation to my beloved Brooklyn and to the friends of four decades from there who continue to enrich my life. You know who you are too! And to the support of three spiritual communities—Congregation Sha'ar Zahav, Kehilla Community Synagogue, and the First Mennonite Church of San Francisco. With special thanks to Lake Merritt in Oakland, around which many of these stories were conceived and gestated. With gratitude to Karen Davis-Faigin, who read though this book with the eyes of an engineer and the ears of a poet. Cantor Sharon Bernstein, who turned the verse of "Ark-less" that I sang into a phone into readable music. Rabbi David Wolpe, for his wonderful blessing-words, and for their invitation to keep studying. San Francisco artist and gallery owner Anne Marguerite Herbst (anneherbst.com) for her painting on the front cover, "Flying Home," and her art on the covers of *Deathless*, *Torah Told Different*, and *Queering the Text*. And with gratitude to everyone at Wipf and Stock who assembled these fragments into a readable object, including:

Jim Tedrick	Managing Editor
Matt Wimer	Assistant Managing Editor
Daniel Lanning	Editorial Assistant

ACKNOWLEDGEMENTS

Stephanie Hough	Typesetter
Ian Creeger	Proofer
Shannon Carter	Cover Design
Dan Crawford	Production
Neil DeBerry	Production
Ryan McGill	Production
Dustin Minder	Production
Nathaniel Stock	Production